Roberts Junction

Kadance Royal

ROYAL MEDIA
& PUBLISHING

Royal Media and Publishing

P. O. Box 4321

Jeffersonville, IN 47131

royalmediapublishing@gmail.com

www.royalmediaandpublishing.com

Originally Released in 2015

Re-released in 2024

ISBN-13: 978-0692548912
ISBN-10: 0692548912
LCCN: 2015914713

Cover Image: Co-Pilot Images

Cover Layout: Elite Book Covers

Printed in the United States of America

List of Characters

Linda Harris Sanders – Worker at Goodwill

John Black – Linda's co-worker at Goodwill

Jamie Miller – Linda's co-worker at Goodwill

Henrietta Mae Robinson – Linda's co-worker at Goodwill

James Sanders – Husband to Linda

William Sanders – Oldest son of Linda and James

Stephen Sanders – Second oldest son of Linda and James

Robert Matthews – First Boyfriend of Linda

Jennifer Brooks – Robert's daughter

Janice Brooks – Robert's daughters' mama

George Bowman – Robert's college friends

Kelli Bowman – George's Wife

Jeremy David Noles – Associate of the Robert Matthews firm – Jamie's first boyfriend

Helen Black – John's mother

Mildred and Bob Jones – John's next-door neighbors

Frank and Martha Miller – Jamie's Parents

The Parkers, Jim, Patty, Ryan and Jason (best friends of William and Stephen) – James and Linda's neighbors

Dedication

This is dedicated to everyone who ever wanted love, thought they were being loved until they found real love.

Kadance

Acknowledgement

The editing staff and creativity of Royal Media and Publishing is to be commended for their ability to broaden the horizons of beginning authors or those entering a new genre with open arms.

Thank you so much.

Table of Contents

Introduction

Sometimes in life, you make long term decisions with short term information.

Linda listened to the bad advice of a high school classmate. That one decision, changed the direction and course of Linda's life.

Robert made one mistake and it cost him the love of his life. He gained a beautiful daughter and a baby mama instead of love and a wife. Would he ever find true love for himself?

Would Linda ever truly live life for herself or would she be stuck in Roberts Junction surviving forever?

Welcome to Roberts Junction. A small town with people who have almost given up on their dreams and love.

One day, one wrong turn and you find yourself living an unhappy life. Another decision, another moment and in an instant, you are filled with love, hope and happiness beyond your wildest dreams.

The people, pain and pleasure of Roberts Junction!

Enjoy!

Chapter 1 - LINDA

"You're just a flat chested, dime store clerk bitch who couldn't get another man if she tried. You better be glad that I married you. I banged your brains out and gave you two wonderful boys. Those are my boys and don't you ever forget it. Your job is to please me and do what I say. I don't beat you even though I could. You just should be glad that I am still with you. There are plenty of women who would want me. I am handsome, smart, well connected in society and come from a long line of lawyers," James Sanders said to his wife Linda. He used to only say it when he was drunk, but these days it was every day. James stood six foot three and weighed two hundred fifty pounds. He was much larger in high school and played on the varsity team. He suffered a knee injury that ended his football hopes in his senior year. His size always was a source of comfort in the beginning of their relationship. Linda was tall at five foot eight and always thin like a model. Linda did not have the model facial beauty. Linda's personality superseded anything she lacked in the looks department. James now used his size to intimidate and belittle Linda. He made her feel small and unworthy of love at all. It was always Linda's fault for it all. Linda sat quietly on the bed not even saying a word or attempting to stand up for herself. She was used to it after 20 years. Her once tall five-foot eight frame was constantly bent over trying to be invisible and protect herself from the constant attacks. The verbal abuse spewed out of James' mouth like thick, stinky vomit covering and diminishing Linda's self-worth day after day. Linda no longer knew James. This was not the fun-loving guy she watched in high school on the football field as she cheered on the side lines. He was not the seemingly supportive and outgoing guy who happened to run into her again at the local junior college in the library. James made her laugh back then. Linda didn't know why she stayed with James. She only knew that this was the boys' father. She hadn't finished college because he promised to give her the world. His family were all lawyers. James always said that he would be a lawyer one day. Instead, he was the office manager at his father's law firm. When he got the letter of rejection from the Indiana University law school, it changed everything. He never got to play football in college. He never got into IU's law school. Of course, it was Linda's fault because she got pregnant and it was a distraction, hindrance and the reason for James' lack of success. That was the beginning of his progression to the next level of abuse, evil and hatred. The pregnancy of William James Sanders was the end of the happy life that James had promised. She wasn't supposed to get pregnant that fast. The doctor's had told her and her mother that she would probably be unable to carry children to full term because her womb was so small. Miracle upon miracles, Linda got pregnant.

At times, Linda allowed herself to remember a happier time. James wasn't the only guy who ever liked her. Robert Matthews was really her first true love. Robert Matthews was gorgeous, fun and smart. He had the softest hair that Linda had ever touched. Robert broke her heart when she found out, that after the Spring Dance, he got drunk at a party and Janice Brooks claimed that Robert got her pregnant. Linda knew that Janice always wanted Robert and would trick him to be with her. The claim became truth and Robert was connected to Janice forever. Just like Linda was connected to James forever by their two boys. To escape James, Linda worked at the local "Goodwill" sorting donated items. The clothes, home furnishings, furniture and appliances were the left overs, cast offs, unwanted and no longer needed items in homes around town. Linda felt unwanted, discarded and not needed on a daily basis by her husband just like these items in the store. Fortunately, her boys, when they were small, always loved and needed her. The two very rambunctious boys kept her on her toes when

James wouldn't take the time or was too busy to spend time with them. Now, they needed her much less. William James Sanders and Stephen Clayton Sanders were young men and the light of her life. William was now entering his sophomore year at Indiana University. Stephen was a senior at the Cedar Ridge High School in Roberts Junction. William plays football and a business major like his dad. Stephen is the star quarterback on the varsity high school football team. Stephen is being heavily recruited by several universities in the area. Linda's weekends are spent at the football field serving on the concession stand, working in the day at the Goodwill, keeping a spotless house and cooking perfect meals for an ungrateful and verbally abusive man. Linda keeps herself looking well in spite of the pain. Linda's hair was still curly and she weighs only 20 pounds different from high school even after birthing two children. James never compliments her appearance, cooking or anything else she does in the house, just constant negativity. Linda felt like it all would never change until one day she and Jamie, Linda's co-worker at Goodwill, were bringing a rack of shirts out onto the sales floor.

"Jamie, I have the rack of shirts and you can bring that small rack of pants over to this rack. We don't have enough for two separate racks so we will put them in order by size on this one rack. Does Ms. Henrietta have any more shirts in the back?" asked Linda. Linda, who was normally silent or only spoke, when necessary, at home, was very verbal at work. Linda spoke up for herself and really was the team leader.

"Linda, give me a second and I will check," Jamie called from the back of the store near the loading and receiving area. As Linda was putting the shirts on the rack, she heard the ringing of the bell on the front door. The bell had been a customer signal for more than 50 years. Prior to the bell, there was always someone at the counter up front. Budget cut backs and technology had eliminated the front door position. Now the bell let all in the building know someone had entered the front door. Unbeknownst to Linda, a man had entered and was now walking toward her.

"Excuse me ma'am," Linda turned quickly to the voice directed very near her. "I am looking for some medium size button down shirts. I have a group of young men that I am working with, and they are trying to find dress shirts to wear on job interviews." Somehow his face looked so familiar even though he was still looking down at the shirts that were already on the rack. The man suddenly turned in Linda's direction and after looking at her face, blinked and said, "Linda Harris Sanders is that you?"

"Yes, I am Linda. Who are you?"

"I am Robert Matthews."

Instantly, Linda dropped her head and began touching her hair. It was the fall of the year but, she hadn't had a hat on so everything was still in place. Linda's mind started racing, 'Robert Matthews and I look a mess. What is he doing in town?' Internally, she chided herself for even having those thoughts. Oh my, 'what would James say?' She knew that James would go on a tangent of ranting and raging about her even speaking to Robert. She could hear him say, 'why were you touching your hair? He's not looking at you or want you. There is nothing special about you!' Linda quickly closed her eyes to blot out the noise of that voice going on inside her head to return to the present conversation with Robert. Robert stood patiently as Linda gathered herself. He was the first to break the silence.

"Are you okay, Linda?"

"I'm sorry. Robert Matthews from high school? Oh, my goodness, how have you been?" Linda asked bringing her attention back to the present.

"I am doing fine. How are you?" Robert continued to look down into Linda's face. He could tell that the years had been kind to her body but not to her face. The lines around her eyes and mouth showed years of wear, tear and frowns because most of the lines turned upside down. James hadn't made her happy after all. Robert was trying not to be judgmental, but he wondered why was Linda was working here? Why isn't she at home or at the country club playing tennis with the other women her age, planning tea parties and bazaars for the school PTA events?

"I am hanging in there. What brings you back in town? You moved away years ago, right?" Linda put one hand on the half empty rack and crossed her feet like in days gone by. Turning to Robert, she tried not to stare. He looked even better now than in high school. The twenty fifth year class reunion was coming soon. Linda had been married a long time but, she could still see. She knew that the forties were looking great on Robert. Robert stood about six foot four with a solid athletic build. He always had soft hair. It was the kind of hair that made you want to touch it while in a long passionate kiss. Why her mind went there, she will never know. Of course, his hair was graying, oh so slightly around his temples which added even more sex appeal. Sex appeal? Linda wished James was sexy. James wasn't sexy, appealing or a master lover at all. What James and Linda did in bed was not anything resembling of love. James would just roll Linda over, handle his business and roll her back over. No foreplay, kisses, intimate touches, soft music, candles or nothing. Linda felt like she was being violated and raped each time. There was no consideration for her feelings, desires or pleasure at all. Linda didn't really know if she had ever had an orgasm in her twenty plus year marriage. Each time she lay there not making a sound. Linda forced herself out of this depressing trance to listen to what Robert had to say.

"Yes, I moved away, but I am now back in Roberts Junction to set up my practice here in addition to my practice in Indianapolis. Are you still married to James?"

"Yes."

"How is he?"

"Fine. So, you say you are setting up a practice here. What kind of practice?" James realized that she only used one word to say how James was doing. He knew that things were as bad as he thought.

"A law practice. I am a lawyer."

"Wow that is fantastic! You always said that you were going to be a lawyer one day."

"Yeah, I did, didn't I?" Robert was looking at the top of Linda's head. After all of this time of wondering, she was actually standing in front of him. He always wondered how things turned out for Linda. Considering where she was working, things hadn't worked that good. Robert continued, "I haven't moved here or setup permanent housing yet. I will be going back and forth between offices until I hire an office manager here in town to run things, hire staff, etc."

She knew what she was about to ask was wrong and really not her place, but here goes nothing, "Are you married?" Linda asked.

"No, I am not married. I have a grown daughter though. Do you remember Janice Brooks?"

"Yes, I believe I do remember Janice," Linda knew she was lying just a bit because she knew Janice 'my boobs, butt and looks' Brooks all too well.

"Janice and I have a daughter together. We are good friends and parents to Jennifer but nothing else. As a matter of fact, Janice is married to someone else."

"Oh, okay," Linda didn't know anything else to say but ok. Conversation outside of the Goodwill was not her strong suit. James didn't talk to her. She didn't have any friends outside of work. She never went out with any adults besides the company picnic, Christmas party and James' parents' house each year. Those business-related events were more like public appearances to put on a good face and make James look good to the other employees and his family.

"Linda, do you have any children?" Linda's eyes lit up, looking straight into Robert's eyes. As a lawyer, Robert was keen to a person's body language, voice changes and facial expressions. Just by her ability to look directly into Robert's face told him that this was a subject that she loved the most and could talk about easily.

"I have two wonderful sons. My oldest is a sophomore at Indiana University Bloomington and plays football like his dad. My youngest is a senior this year at the high school and plays football as well."

"I know that James is proud of his sons, too." At the mention of James, Linda dropped her head again.

"Yeah, I guess so."

Just then a voice came from behind Linda. A rack of shirts was being navigated by Jamie which interrupted their conversation. The rack of shirts was taller than Jamie so she didn't see that Linda was in a conversation with Robert or that he was even standing there.

"Linda, here are the remaining sorted and tagged shirts that you wanted."

Linda turned toward the voice. Jamie was talking and walking so that she almost ran into the back of Linda. Robert slightly touched Linda's right shoulder reaching around her to stop the rack before it got too close.

"Watch out, Jamie!" Linda called out. Jamie stopped abruptly and looked up into the very handsome man's face.

"I am sorry, Linda. I didn't see anybody standing there besides you because the rack was blocking. Excuse me sir, who are you?" Jamie said in her very flirty voice.

Before Robert could answer, Linda stopped her.

"Um, are there any other shirts in the back?"

"No, I don't think so," Her eyes going up and down Robert's built to please frame. 'This man is simply gorgeous and why is he talking to Linda? I will have to find out at lunch.' Jamie thought to herself.

"Jamie, why don't you go to the back and just double-check," Linda was giving Jamie the eye to go on. Jamie was the gossiper and the most inquisitive one of the group. Jamie hesitantly walked away from them both.

"Robert, you asked me about shirts?" Turning quickly away from Jamie's eyes.

"Yes."

"Well, here they are. What size do you need?" Linda said nervously touching and moving shirts quickly on the round rack.

"I need various sizes to fit young men."

"You are buying for a group of young men that are teenagers you say?"

"Yes, my company is committed to mentoring. Some of them are interested in being lawyers one day or just a viable member of society." Robert was looking down to make eye contact with Linda. Because of Linda's height, her eyes never came higher than his neck.

"That is wonderful," Linda said thinking about her own boys.

"Yes, it is wonderful. We have been participating in this program for about 3 years. We find that we have to help them with some of their basic needs before they can move forward in such a demanding profession. We want to equip these young people, so, we give them the knowledge, tools and uniform of sorts to dress the part. They need shirts, so here I am," Robert chuckled slightly and awkwardly. He began looking through the shirts again. There were so many questions running through his mind that he thought it would be best to just pick out some shirts. He picked out several solid shirts and only a few that had a print pattern. The legal field still has a very traditional dress code for men and women.

"I try to tell my boys, all of the time, that a good education is key to being able to be great husbands, friends, providers and fathers to their children one day. James works a lot and not able to spend much time with them so I do as much as I can," Linda face suddenly lit up again when she mentioned her sons.

"That's awesome. I can tell that you love your sons and are a great mother, Linda." Robert knew by Linda's words that her heart was into her sons.

"I try."

"Well, look at the time. I need to get these shirts so I can make a meeting at Sanders & Associates."

"Well, that's James' family firm and he works there. He is the office manager," Linda said nervously. She felt herself rambling. She hoped that Robert wouldn't mention that he had seen or talked to her at the store.

"I may stop in and say hi. How do I check out and pay for the shirts?"

"Oh, I can check you out. I don't see Jamie or John." Robert followed Linda to the checkout counter to pay for his goods. They conversed idly as he gathered his receipt and said goodbye.

Jamie was standing in the back looking through the small, round, clear panels in the swinging doors in the back. "Why are you standing there meddling and doing nothing? You are so nosy." John another employee had walked upon Jamie and she nearly jumped out of her skin at his voice.

"John! You nearly scared me to death," Jamie said.

"I should have scared you because you are wasting time on the clock meddling in other people's conversation," John replied.

"I am not wasting time at all. I am trying to figure out who that man is that Linda has been talking to so long. He seems to be very interested in her. I haven't seen her smile that much in a long time. Who is he?" Jamie asked.

"I keep forgetting that you haven't lived in Roberts Junction that long. That is Robert Matthews. He went to high school with Linda and her husband James. He played football with James. I just heard at the barber shop that he is moving back into town to open a law practice and hopefully, compete with Sanders & Associates. They've been the only law firm in town for many years. I am not saying they aren't good, but sometimes being the only game in town is just not good. It doesn't give you any options."

"Oh, okay. Were they high school sweethearts?" Jamie asked.

"Yes, I think so. I don't know really what happened to give Linda a reason to marry James but, she is married and probably not interested in Robert Matthews," John said.

A slow smile started on Jamie's face, "Married or not, I'd be interested in someone that good-looking. I can't wait to tease her and ask her more about this Robert Matthews at lunch later."

"Stop acting like you are trying to fix up a girlfriend for prom. Leave Linda alone. I watched 'em the whole time, the conversation was harmless," John chided.

"Yeah, it was harmless alright but, they have history. Speaking of wasting time, look at you standing here watching too," Jamie added.

Jamie couldn't wait for Linda to come to the back for lunch. The Goodwill workers ate together from 12-1 and old man Harrison came in to man the store during the lunch hour.

"Listen, don't you get nothing started with your nosy self. The good book says that you shouldn't come between married people or nothing," John said.

"But I wonder if she is happily married?" Jamie began to muse.

"Is that really any of your business if she is happy or not? She is still married. Are you happy with your life?" John asked.

"Yeah, I am happy as long as I am meddling in somebody else's business," Jamie looked up at John and smiled like a sly fox.

"I can see that. You are pathetic. Come away from that door and tell me where you guys left off back here with sorting. After lunch, I want to get started right away." John walked away from the door immediately. Jamie continued to watch the exchange between Linda and Robert. 'This is going to be interesting,' Jamie thought to herself.

"Well, Linda, it's been good seeing you again and talking with you." Robert was looking at Linda one more time to take her all in. He couldn't believe that Linda was standing right in front of him. He had thought all along that Linda and James would have moved away after high school. Linda was looking down and not looking directly into Robert's eyes hoping that he couldn't see directly into her soul.

"Thanks. It's good seeing you too. Have a great day." Her eyes landed somewhere in his chest area as she handed him his bag of shirts.

"You too. If I need more shirts, I may see you again soon," Robert said as he walked out the front door. Linda smiled a half smile as he left. The bell rang on the door as it closed. Linda made the mistake of continuing to watch out the front door as Robert got in his car. She tried not to let her mind wander. Seeing and talking to Robert again brought back memories of 'what if' and 'what could have been.' She had made her choice and would have to live with it. Linda knew that just seeing Robert opened up something that should have remained closed. She couldn't stand here wondering, wishing and wanting for another life she didn't have because she had a lunch to eat and more work to do.

In the meantime, Robert left the Goodwill, shirts safely on the front seat and headed straight toward Sanders & Associates. He wanted to do a friendly meet and greet with the office manager and/or partners with that firm considering he was setting up a practice as well. He knew it was risky coming back home to such a small town that already had a law firm, but he had his reasons. The office was only 2 blocks from the Goodwill. Robert opened his car, threw the bag inside and walked to Sanders and Associates. Roberts Junction had only a few shops on Main Street. The funeral home, court house, barber shop, a dry goods store and a diner or two. On the outskirts of town near the highway, was a Waffle House, McDonalds, a couple of larger banks and a Super Walmart. Robert didn't know what small town America would do if Walmart didn't exist.

Robert walked in the wood front door with Sanders & Associates in gold letters on the window. He noticed that there was no receptionist on duty. There was no bell or tone that sounded, no security cameras and apparently, no care. Wow, yes, he was back in a small town. He had worked at so many law firms, he could surely find his way around this one. There was a young lady walking toward him and he assumed that she was the receptionist. He was wrong. She turned down a hallway before she reached him before he could ask her for the office manager. A young man who appeared to be delivering mail came toward him, and Robert stopped him.

"Excuse me young man, where is Mr. Sanders, the office manager?" Robert asked.

"His office is straight ahead and turn left down the next hall and his office is all of the way at the end of the hallway," said the young man.

"Thanks so much." Robert proceeded down the hallway. There were phones ringing, keyboards clicking madly and people marching between offices with manila folders in their hands. The door said, 'Office Manager.' Robert knocked lightly but, no answer. He tried the door and it was unlocked. When he opened the door, he saw a man sitting behind his desk, head back in the chair, eyes closed and making moaning sounds. Because of the carpet, the man was totally unaware that Robert had entered the room. He could see a young woman's head going up and down on her knees apparently giving him the blow job of his life.

Robert was going to watch for a while, but decided against it, he said, "Excuse me but, are you James Sanders?"

"You stupid bitch, you didn't lock the door!" James grabbed his pants together and then stood up from his chair slightly in order to close them.

The young woman made a low, surprised scream, jumped up and ran out of the room repeating, "I'm sorry, so sorry," as she closed the door behind her.

"What the hell do you want?"

"It's apparent that I don't have to ask you what you want, James. I take it that was the receptionist that wasn't at the desk when I came in the front door."

"Right."

"Well, I was stopping by as a mere courtesy visit to let you know that I will be establishing a branch office here in Roberts Junction. I try to play nice unless I am provoked. I left a message with your secretary. Didn't she tell you or did you have other duties for her to attend to?"

"Funny. She probably did, but I forgot. Why do you want an office here in Roberts Junction? I know that you are doing well in Indianapolis."

"Business is booming so I thought I would come home to Roberts Junction and allow them to enjoy some of the fruit of my labor. Apparently, something you know little about," Robert added.

"Funny." James made a hissing sound between his teeth cocking his head slightly to the side, rolling his eyes and aimed them right at Robert.

"Don't act nasty with me. I wasn't just caught with my pants down literally. Wouldn't your father love to know that. By the way, how many times have you left the door unlocked and been caught or almost caught? Also, that is somebody's daughter that was just performing that act on you. In the workplace, really? Too cheap for a hotel?" Robert had an image of his poor wife, Linda's face. He realized that he should keep this little secret to himself until it was absolutely necessary.

Robert turned and left with James' blank, silent stare still on his face.

Chapter 2 - John

'Remember, you will always be Mommy's baby boy. I would die without you helping me. Now, will you go to the grocery and pick up these items for me? I gave birth to you. You know that your father walked out on me. You are the only one that will take care of me now. With that talk of moving out and living your own life, are you trying to kill your mother?' John had heard these words over and over again every day for the past thirty years. He loved his mother and wanted only what was best for her. Since his father left with the high school English teacher for Atlanta, it had been this way. John was now his mother's everything. He was her replacement husband, caregiver, friend and provider too. His mother used all types of excuses on John. She was depressed, sad, worried, heart broken or that she wasn't smart enough to get a job and support herself. The truth was that she weak and always wanted someone to care for her. John's father wasn't that type of man that would just dote on or pamper one person. He was progressive and desired to be a mover and shaker in society. Helen was content to stay at home forever waiting on someone to bring her food, clothing and news from the outside world. John couldn't bring himself to abandon his mother. So, he worked two jobs to care for his mother. He had worked third shift at the Ford plant in Louisville, KY and then part-time at the Goodwill in the morning just to keep busy. He hated to think that he worked that much to get away from his mother, but he did. She was suffocating him. She was smothering him. She was keeping him from living. She poured everything that probably was intended for his father on to him. He didn't want to think that she ran his father away but deep inside he knew that she did. From the day that John's father left Roberts Junction, he never returned. He never sent Christmas cards, birthday presents, came to his high school graduation or when he graduated from trade school. John knew how to get in touch with his father. John's father was in the paper countless times for winning some award, having some honor bestowed or achieving some success with his new wife and children. John knew that he would always be his mother's son, but he wanted to be someone's husband, lover and friend. He had had some dates over the years but, nothing serious because of his mother. He wasn't good looking but, 'easy on the eyes' as one woman had put it. He stood six foot four and weighed a healthy two hundred twenty-five pounds. He was a regular guy in work clothes, nothing fancy. He rarely went to a wedding, formal dinner or anywhere that he would have to dress up. He worked so much lifting heavy equipment and boxes that going to the gym was unnecessary. The work produced the effect of sculpturing his body into great form. There were times when he yearned for a woman so bad that he would meet one at a hotel just for the evening. He couldn't spend the night or his mother would blow up his phone. He tried once to stay all night but ended up taking the woman home at 3:00 a.m. just to satisfy his mother. This angered the woman so much that she never spoke or saw him again. It was apparent that none of John's needs mattered to his mother, just her own needs. Once a woman asked him if he were gay since he never had a woman around. He quickly replied, "No." He totally understood her asking because at nearly fifty years old, what was he waiting on? John realized that his desire to please his mom dashed any hopes of loving and pleasing anyone else. She wanted to be first place, number one in his life, forever.

John kept promising himself that he was going to retire soon from Ford and just work part-time at the Goodwill when he met a nice woman. Until he met that special someone, he worked both jobs. Because he worked so much, took care of his mother and didn't go out much, he hadn't met that someone special. It was a cycle that continued day after day.

Jamie and John were still standing in the door way when Linda headed to the back of the store from the checkout counter with Robert Matthews.

"Here she comes." Jamie was the first to run away from the door way and head to the break room. John kept watching Linda as she walked toward the door. John had worked with Linda long enough to notice a new look on Linda's face. He had never seen it before until today. It's that faraway look in her eyes mixed with intermittent smiles, long glances at nothingness. It was that yearning, longing and remembering what could have been or should have been. John had known Linda and Robert since they lived in Roberts Junction. Even though he was much older than Linda, Robert and James, it was a small town and the entire town came to high school events especially the games, plays and carnivals. He attended many of these events to get away from his mother on many occasions. He went alone just to observe people and live vicariously through other people's lives. He used to imagine him having a wife and children going to one of these school events together. He dreamed of his freedom one day, but how and when? He really didn't want his mom to die for him to enjoy life, but time was slipping by so quickly. John turned fifty this year. How much longer would he have to wait? He was getting older and didn't want to be too old to enjoy any pleasure with a woman. Any longer, he would have to find someone who would be content to be held, cuddled and stroked. That was no fun. He wanted to use his last bit of virility with a woman he could love, cherish, appreciate, and she would respond in like passion with the same love and appreciation for him. He had to get his mind off of his problems and focus on the work at hand. He soon moved away from the door to allow Linda to push the swinging door open.

Jamie moved toward Linda quickly. "So, who was the handsome man you were talking to earlier?"

"Leave her alone, Jamie," John reminded.

"I'm not trying to mess with her too much just a little teasing in good fun," Jamie said with a very wide smile.

"What are you talking about Jamie?" Linda asked.

"As Ms. Henrietta would say, that tall glass of good-looking drinking water you were talking to earlier?"

"Just a classmate from high school," Linda said while emptying her lunch bag.

"I hear it is more than just a classmate from high school. Was he your high school sweetheart?" Jamie asked.

"No, not really, oh well, yeah I guess so," Linda said sounding a bit confused herself. She was taken aback by everything that had happened today as a whole. Robert is back in town is all that kept going through her mind.

"You guess so, was he, or wasn't he?" Jamie inquired further.

"I guess he was. Robert was the guy I dated right before James," Linda stated.

"Listen at you sounding like the evening news investigative reporter or better yet a cross examiner. Stop it already Jamie. Linda is not one bit single. She is very married. Stop acting like a school girl trying to fix your girlfriend up with a guy for prom," John scolded.

"I'm not. I just wanted to have a little fun," Jamie smiled again.

"Yeah right. You've had enough fun for one day. Let it go." John rolled his eyes because he knew Jamie was a meddler. She meddled into everybody's business in the store. She was always poking her nose where it didn't belong. He often wondered what she really had going on in her life that made her want to know what others were doing. Jamie had only been in Roberts Junction for ten years and just showed up to the Goodwill one day looking for a job. She didn't have references, but there was a job open and she said that she could work so Steve hired her. She didn't talk much at first, but over time she warmed up to everyone in the store. The only thing was that she really didn't fit in with the small-town people. She stuck out just a little. She had big city ways. She liked high fashion magazines and bought them often. Even when she first arrived, her clothes would have been in the name brand section of the store and not the discount brands.

He had learned from his mother that when someone is unhappy with their life, they seek to involve themselves in and control the life of others. If he ever got the chance or the nerve, he would never, ever let someone control his life again. He would live life to the fullest and do more than just work but live. When would that day come? How would he ever be free to just live? What would he do with the freedom that he so longed for? He didn't know, but one thing for sure he was going to keep living until he found it for himself. He was also dying to know Jamie's story.

Chapter 3 - Jamie

"You let this Noles boy put his dick in you!" Jamie's father was screaming to the top of his lungs.

"Honey, calm down, you know what the doctor said about your heart." Jamie's mother tried to sooth and make him calm down with the sound of her voice.

"Screw the doctor, I will not calm down when a daughter of mine goes and has sex in a park on the top of a truck like an animal. Really Jamie? Do you not have any more pride about yourself than that? I could see if you were inside the car, at least you would be protected from the elements but outside like a common low life, poor white trash without money enough to get a room, whore. You had a car! Why couldn't you have stayed in it? The officer said your ass was mooning the world like a rabbit. You were charged with indecent exposure, and fortunately, David is not eighteen or I would have his ass under the jail. Charm school and all the private school money we dished out didn't teach you nothing with that hot ass of yours. Martha, she must get that from your side of the family. Your daddy was truly a rolling stone." Jamie's mother, Martha, whipped her head around at Frank with such disgust that he knew that he was going to be hearing about this for at least six months if not a year.

Jamie Miller and Jeremy Noles were sitting on the couch in the living room of the Miller's home on the receiving end of some very cruel, rude, insulting, but true statements from Jamie's father. Jamie and David were caught in the act of having sex in the park on top of his pick-up truck on the wrong side of the tracks. It was a summer night. One thing led to another while they were laying on a blanket on the roof of his truck. Then the bright lights and siren from the police car were turned on, the bull horn sounded tell them to 'stop.' They were trying to find their clothes by the blinding police car light to cover themselves. There were no drugs and they hadn't been drinking so Jamie was brought home by Indianapolis' finest. The charges were immediately dropped. David followed Jamie home because he really cared about her. He also knew how much trouble she was in, and he didn't want her to take it alone. He was also on top of that pick-up truck.

Jamie wouldn't call it love exactly, but she cared about David too. Even though he didn't have all of the things she had access to, he was a nice guy. His family worked and wasn't on public assistance. They lived in a trailer, but it was a double wide, nice and clean on the inside. Jamie believed that David liked her for who she was and not for what her family money could buy. She was spoiled but smart. She got good grades in school but really didn't like to follow the rules. That was her down fall. What teenager wouldn't love to have a car, clothes, a bank account replenished each month, a credit card with no limit and a drawer in the kitchen with cash money for her wallet every week? Jamie. After that night with David, it wasn't enough. Her parents demanded that Jamie never see David again, and she didn't. But Jamie went from bad to worse. She started going after the bad boys and encountering one bad relationship after another. She began making terrible decisions in all areas of her life. Her life of luxury and ease wasn't enough to make her follow the rules. She went to college and still got into trouble. She was smart enough to know, that if her father decided to, he would make good on his threats to cut off her bank account, credit cards and other allowances to keep her in line. So, she became sneaky and withdrew the money from her account and opened a new account in another bank not associated with her family. The statements were sent to a post office box in a small neighboring town which Jamie checked monthly. Her escapades with bad boys landed her in some terrible places like honkey tonk bars, strip clubs and even crack houses.

Finally, all of the poor living and choices came to a head on a horrible Saturday night. The latest boyfriend was Barry. He was excitement on steroids. He liked fast cars, drugs, fighting and beating Jamie. The beatings happened a few times but, she kept coming back for more. The initial fun and laughs turned south when Barry decided to try out the drugs that he was selling. It started off as a dare, but in spite of all he had seen, he still tried it. He became addicted so fast that he was barely keeping up with the payments to his supplier because he was using so much of the product instead of selling it. That stash of cash that Jamie had accumulated funded this sick, co-dependent relationship. Barry became violent with everyone around him to get what his body craved. The drugs took over. Jamie left time and time again, but kept coming back. She didn't feel like she had any place to go. Jamie was stealing anything to put food on the table. There was a line that she wouldn't cross, but a purse nearby was fair game. Thank goodness that condoms and birth control were free or she surely would have been pregnant and having to figure that situation out too. Finally, one night she had had enough and she tried to leave him. This time it would have to be for good. Secretly, she had been going to the gun range to learn how to protect herself from Barry as well as any other intruder. Barry had bought her the first gun a long time ago. Jamie refused to carry the gun at first but changed her mind when she had to use the gun to bluff her way out of a lot of crazy situations that Barry had gotten her in. Jamie realized now that she was fighting for her life. They were living in a walk-up apartment on the second floor on the west side of Indianapolis. Barry liked living on the second floor. He could post a look out on the first floor or just look out the window to give him a warning if the cops were coming or another enemy so he could get out through the fire escape. The rent was due, there was no food in the refrigerator, and her last bit of savings was long gone. The cable was cut off because it went for the last hit. Having no job or access to money was no longer fun. When Barry was high, he wasn't interested in doing anything but, getting to the next high. Jamie's job was to just sit and watch him destroy himself. Being wild was fun for a while but reality had finally set in.

"Bitch where you think you going?" Barry looked at Jamie with a snarl and slight sniff after snorting $300 worth of cocaine. Jamie had grabbed her purse, jacket and an overnight bag she had packed earlier. She was almost out the door. She thought Barry was out, but she waited too long and he woke up.

"Barry, you scared me." Jamie immediately jumped at the sound of his voice and turned to see exactly where he was to move quickly in case of another attack. He had already beaten her earlier for not wanting to give him the last bit of money she stole from an old lady at the grocery store. The old lady turned her back too long and her purse was open with her wallet and coupons. Jamie knew she was in trouble and couldn't put her back to him and run. She was going to have to stand her ground and fight. Even now, he was too strong for her to avoid him.

"I have had enough and I want to go home. We have been down this road too many times. I am tired, hungry and broke. I have not been happy in months. Let me go!" Jamie's voice was quivering and she was trying to back into the doorway, grab the handle and turn the knob to get out.

"You are home, bitch, and I intend to keep you here no matter what. I don't care nothing about you being happy. You owe me, and you are going to pay dearly. You are not going to leave me by myself!"

"No, Barry I have got to leave. I don't know where I am going, but I've got to get the hell out of here." Barry moved quickly toward her, grabbed her by the hair, spun her around and penned her to the door. To Jamie, it seemed to be in one swift motion. His bad breath, stench of not bathing and smell of smoke was overwhelming.

"You think you're going to live it up on me for all of these months and then walk out on me when I'm down? I'll be back up in a little bit. I just need to get my shit together and I will be fine."

"No, you need some help. You let me out, and I will get the help you need," Jamie pleaded.

"You are not going anywhere." Barry slapped her and she fell to her knees to the floor. The beating that commenced was the worst ever. Black, blue and blood were mixed in with insults, swearing and more fighting. Jamie realized that if she was going to make it out of this alive, she was going to have to do something drastic. The last time she landed on the floor she slid and landed near her purse. Barry was resting up against the doorway. Jamie knew that Barry was unarmed because he was in his underwear and t-shirt. Her body was laying still but, her hands were working feverishly to get the gun out her purse for the next round. She thought, 'No more hitting me. My father never hit me so why would I let this guy keep hitting me. He has nothing and is not headed toward nothing either.' Barry came off the wall one more time but was stopped by the pointed gun.

"Look at you. Got a gun and now you think you all bad. You don't know how to use that thing," Barry said smugly.

"Try me bastard! I have had enough of you hitting me. Don't take another step or I..." Jamie stopped short.

"Or you will do what? You gonna shoot me? Barry 'keeping everybody merry' me?" Barry stumbled closer taking two shaky steps closer.

"Don't come closer please. I don't want to just shoot you. I want to kill your ass!" Jamie was screaming now and knew that this was it. Barry came two more steps closer. She pulled the trigger the first time and the bullet hit Barry in the stomach. He was as strong as an ox so he kept walking closer and closer. She knew that it was all over for her if she let him grab her. So, Jamie kept firing the gun until he landed face down at her feet. The police sirens were heard coming down the street. She knew that jail would be her home for life. Jamie was immediately arrested and taken into custody. The police knew that it was a domestic violence case by the emergency call. The body of the victim was lying dead in a pool of blood on the floor from apparent gunshot wounds. Through the blood, bruises and disarray of the apartment from the apparent fight, the real victim was this young woman. The judge and jury would have to decide that. It was now time for Jamie to face the music. Her only hope was to contact her parents.

"Daddy?" Jamie's dad answered the phone reluctantly at 2:00 a.m. on a Saturday night.

"Jamie? Is this you? What do you want?"

"Daddy, I am in some real trouble. I need your help."

"Where are you?"

"County jail."

"Jail? Are you kidding me? What are you doing in jail?" Jamie began to tell her father the entire story. In the end, he said that he would send an attorney in the morning to check on things.

Over the next several months, Jamie endured a highly publicized trial with the news media camped everywhere from the courtroom to her parents' home. They reported every new development, every single day of the defense and prosecution side of the case. The best lawyer money could buy was hired to defend Jamie. In Johnny Cochran style, her daddy's money bought her freedom. What would she do with this new found freedom?

"Jamie, your father and I need to talk to you. Get dressed and meet us at the breakfast table," Jamie's mother said as she turned on the bedroom light, walked to the bed and slightly shook it. It had been more than five years since Jamie had slept in this bed or been in her room. Her memorabilia from school still hung on the walls but, only a few important pieces. The remaining old papers, notebooks and unnecessary stuff had been put away in the attic or thrown away. Her clothes were already washed and laid out on her chair at her desk just like her mom had taught her as a child. 'Always prepare yourself the night before for the next day,' Mom always said. Jamie thought she would be able to stay with her parents for the next several months to get a job, back on her feet and build some kind of quality life for herself. It was not to be so. Jamie's father had the perfect plan devised for Jamie. When she came to the dining room, breakfast was on the table along with two envelopes. Jamie was sitting in a chair positioned in the middle of the table and her parents were on either end like those two book ends. She remembered all of those years of this sitting arrangement at the table. The feel of the room let Jamie know that her parents were serious and this was important. Jamie sat down and took a sit a juice before her father started.

"Jamie, you will find two envelopes on the table. One has a bus ticket to anywhere you want to go. The second envelope has $10,000 to get you started in any city in this country.

You cannot stay here with us. You have embarrassed your mother and me to the limit. We will always love you, but you have got to go. Eat your breakfast, pack your things and we will take you to the bus station at 11:00 a.m. The bus schedule is wide open at that time. Let us know where you are settling. Feel free to call back and visit for the holidays. With the media attention you have gained, you have got to go." Her mother wiped a tear, but didn't break down at Jamie's father's words. Her mother didn't like it but, it could not be helped.

"I understand. I am so sorry for all of the pain and shame that I have caused you both. I thank you for all of your help throughout this mess I caused in my life. But, one day I hope to make you very proud of me." Jamie finished eating in silence. There was smooth jazz playing in the background to somehow sooth the pain of this new rough transition in Jamie's life. Which city to go to? Where should she start over? The big city or a small one? Those were the questions in Jamie's mind as she headed to the bus station. Upon their arrival, her parents said goodbye and drove off leaving Jamie standing alone looking at the schedule. Suddenly, she realized that she had been recognized and people were staring. The bus station is not usually where paparazzi or anybody famous would hang out. Jamie wasn't a celebrity but, she had become known from the news. People started coming in close and started asking questions.

"Aren't you that girl who killed that guy and got off?" Others just pointed, whispered or mumbled, "I think that's her" or "wonder why she is here in the bus station. I know her people are rich."

The decision of where to go was taken out of her hands. She ran toward a bus and got on. Jamie didn't know that the bus that she had just boarded wasn't going that far away from Indianapolis but to Louisville, KY. Because of the confusion, the driver got on and announced that he would look at their tickets one block away from the station. This was quite unusual but, the crowd was forming fast and growing in numbers. The bus took off in a hurry.

After the excitement of the crowd, you would think that would be enough, but no. The bus broke down about 30 miles outside of Louisville. A school bus arranged by the bus company took them to nearby Roberts Junction of all places. The passengers boarded the school bus and another bus brought their luggage. This whole practice was unusual. The passengers were fussing and outdone to have to be towed and go to another city. The repair of the bus was critical to resuming the trip. It wasn't like they were in no man's land, just off I-65, but the situation was out of their hands.

Jamie was looking at this small town as the bus went down Main Street. There was a Goodwill, a barber shop, a beauty salon, a hardware store and the courthouse. The post office was next and then a few other business establishments. A Walmart was just off the highway. There were a couple of banks, churches and community center. Jamie was always impulsive, that's how she had gotten into so much trouble. She thought she was going to hide out in a big city. What if she came to the small city? Usually, small towns asked a lot of questions but, she had lied before, she could lie again. With practice, she would try to fit it instead of hiding out in the big city. Jamie realized that she had been through enough and decided she wanted to turn over a new leaf. There was a hiring sign on the Goodwill door. If you were leaving the repair shop, you were to leave your cell number with the bus driver. Jamie didn't leave a cell phone number but left the building. She walked across the street to the Goodwill store with no luggage to retrieve only a new life to start building.

Today, years after crossing the street into the Goodwill store, Jamie is still here. Steve is at the counter as usual while John, Jamie and Linda are in the break room. John works 4-

5 hours a day for 3 days a week or it would interfere with his retirement. Linda and Jamie are the only two full-time employees.

"So, Linda, when are you headed to the game to see your son play this weekend at IU?" Jamie asked.

"I am going up on Friday and probably spend the night. IU plays Purdue. It is going to be a great game. I am so proud of William," Linda said smiling.

"You should be proud. You have two wonderful boys. But you should be careful because they said it's going to snow. This is the first snow of the season. Do you want me to ride with you?" Jamie prodded just a little because she really did care about Linda and her safety. In Indiana, a snow storm could happen at any time. One minute, it is all clear and the next 5 miles, you could have zero visibility and ice on the roads. Jamie also knew that it would be another weekend alone in her small apartment watching old movies, football, popcorn and game shows. She couldn't bring herself to go out even across the bridge to Louisville to a club or bar because she just might meet the wrong guy. She couldn't face that again. She had built a prison of her own in Roberts Junction and at the Goodwill with the only friends she had left. Her old friends from high school wouldn't want to know the current Jamie without her parents' money and status. Her friends from the streets were either dead or in jail. A football game with one friend might have been nice. To do something different over the weekend would have been a great change. Why Linda wanted to be alone, Jamie didn't know, but she wanted her friend to be careful and return on Monday.

"No, really, I want to go by myself. It gives me peace and quiet from everything. If I get snowed in, I will check into a hotel or stay in the dorm with William." Linda knew she needed a relief from everything and everybody.

"Just be careful my friend. I want to see you back here on Monday safe and sound," Jamie said.

"I will, don't worry." Tears almost formed in Linda's eyes to know that someone actually cared about her. Linda knew that James didn't care about her at all. Linda felt like her sons loved her, but James could care less. Linda only admitted James' verbal abuse to herself. James was a grown man. He had made his choices on how he would behave, and at present, he wasn't going to change. Their marriage was one of inconvenience. They never rode together to any of the boys' activities. James came to both William and Stephen's football, baseball or basketball games late and usually left early. He made sure that he made a great showing to the other parents, their coaches and to the boys while they were on the sidelines or the bench. Once he yelled their name out, got their attention and waved, he stayed a few minutes and then left. Linda wasn't stupid. She knew that James was going somewhere, but where and with whom, she didn't know. She really didn't want to know. She just wanted him to leave her alone. She knew that she was taking her life in her hands every time that he had sex with her. Linda hoped that James used protection when he was with someone else, but how was she to know. Linda thought she could deal with James if he were silent, but James didn't care anything about Linda. He stayed married to her for her maid service and to keep up with his brothers who had wives and children. He had lost so much; he didn't want to lose his sons. James' father had made sure that his children understood the importance of family, good or bad, normal or dysfunctional. Family is everything. On the other hand, Linda didn't leave him either. She could have left and started over somewhere but, with what? She had no house or car that she had bought on her own. She had worked at the Goodwill. The job was respectable but, what do you do with little saved and no real plan for the future? She hid a little money in a shoe box in her underwear drawer but, what was that really in the full scheme of things financially? With her youngest son a senior in high school, if James had been the right man, she should be planning for retirement in a few years. So many questions and so many scary answers. Linda knew that she didn't deserve this life and one day something would have to change or she would go insane. How would she do this to her family? What would be the final straw that break the camel's back and set her free? Linda couldn't wrap her mind around the possibility. So, for now, she would keep up the façade until change finally came.

"That should be a good game on Saturday, Linda. I will be watching it on TV, of course, with my mom," John chimed in and embarrassed because that was his ending in most statements, 'with my mom.' John loved football. He would have enjoyed going to a game or two in Bloomington with a group of guys along with their wives or girlfriends. That was impossible to think about because he just couldn't leave his mom. John looked at the clock and knew that Ms. Henrietta would soon be walking in the door. It was her day to join them. Ms. Henrietta was employed here when John got hired. He knew that he would never know her whole story, but who really did?

Chapter 4 - Ms. Henrietta

"Good afternoon, everybody." A now wrinkled, but still stately lady came into the Goodwill from the back loading dock. It was Ms. Henrietta Robinson.

'Good afternoon, Ms. Henrietta or hello Ms. Henrietta,' were all greetings from the other employees at the Goodwill.

"Alright Ms. Jamie, tell me what's going on today since you are always the one with the news." Ms. Henrietta always wore a uniform of either white, black or gray. Today, she had on a gray uniform. Her uniform was pressed with creases along the sleeves, across the back at her shoulder blades and down the front that looked like seams instead of pressed creases. Ms. Henrietta always told the employees there, 'look your best, act your best and you will get the best.' Ms. Henrietta didn't care that the place was a Goodwill, she was going to look her best.

"Well, Linda had an old boyfriend from high school come in to the store from Indianapolis. He is a lawyer and getting ready to open an office here in Roberts Junction. He used to live here years ago from what I can tell. That's all I know so far." Jamie turned from Ms. Henrietta toward Linda with a smile.

"There you go again, assuming and nosing into other people's business," John reminded Jamie for the third time that day.

"Ms. Henrietta wasn't here earlier, and she asked me about what's going on so I told her." Jamie continued to smile at John who definitely was not smiling, but frowning at Jamie imposing herself yet again. She not only meddled with Linda but revealed things about customers.

Linda didn't say anything in response to Jamie. She just kept her head down and continued to eat her sandwich, chips and soda. It was pointless to try to combat that mouth of Jamie's. Linda was a bit confused, herself, how she felt about Robert coming into the store today. She didn't want to think about it but, over the past hour she wondered what would have happened if she had just waited a little longer. What if she hadn't been so gullible and fallen prey to the advances of James, where would she be today? Linda couldn't think about that. She had to get her mind ready to deal with James once he got home, pack her a bag for her trip to Bloomington for her son's game and get gas on the way home so she wouldn't have to fill up on her way out of town.

Ms. Henrietta noticed that Linda was quiet, "Are you okay Linda? You are awful quiet over there, honey. I am sure that Jamie was just teasing you."

"Yes, Ms. Henrietta, I am fine. Just got a lot on my mind."

"Well, honey if you want to talk about it, you know where I am. Don't let Jamie get to you. If you can survive Jamie's teasing, you can survive anything."

"Almost anything," Linda replied. Ms. Henrietta wanted to inquire what Linda meant by that statement, but she knew that too many ears were around. Many years ago, Linda and Ms. Henrietta worked alone at the Goodwill. Ms. Henrietta knew that Linda didn't share every detail of her life and neither had she. She could always tell that a lot was going on when Linda didn't join into the conversation. Ms. Henrietta knew what it was like to keep secrets. She had kept a lot of her own secrets over the past 70 years of her life.

If anyone worked in the Goodwill and kept their eyes open, they would realize that all of the employees of the Goodwill in Roberts Junction had their own secrets. Underneath all of the secrets was a bondage or a hold to something or to someone. These bondages were keeping all of them from living their best life. John was bound to his mother. Jamie was still bound by her past and remained stuck here in Roberts Junction too lazy or scared to move forward. Jamie could have moved to another city or state with no husband or children, but it was easier to stay here. Jamie didn't trust her own judgment of people. There was safety just being alone. Linda, of course, was bound by her commitment to her sons by staying with their father and keeping up the façade of a family, dysfunctional as it was. Ms. Henrietta had her own bondage to Roberts Junction by the choices she had made long ago.

Ms. Henrietta only worked 3-4 hours a day for 2 days from March to October because she was retired and didn't like to come out in the winter. At least that's what Ms. Henrietta told everybody. In actuality, Ms. Henrietta didn't have to work.

Years ago, Ms. Henrietta's worked for the Walker family in the big white house on the corner of Main and Branch Streets in the heart of the town. Ms. Henrietta was the Negro housekeeper, maid or day worker which ever you wanted to call her. She worked for Mr. Jefferson and Mrs. Mary Walker 3 days a week and an extra day when they were going to have company. Ms. Henrietta dusted, vacuumed, cooked, cleaned the windows, did the grocery shopping and polished silver. There were two things that Ms. Henrietta didn't do, take care of children and say no to Mr. Walker.

You would think that without children that Mrs. Walker would keep her own house, but if your husband was prominent in a city or town, you didn't clean your own house. Along with the other bridge club or country club wives, you helped to plan tea parties, socials and compared notes on supervising a Negro or black housekeeper. This was a carryover from slavery. Even in a small town, the Jim Crow laws, segregation and respect for white people was the law. Slavery was over, but black people still weren't free. They were either bound by illiteracy, poverty or opportunity. The idea of a Negro, colored, black or an African American U. S. President would have had the forefathers of this nation rolling over in their graves. The idea of inter-racial marriages is very prominent in recent years, but in the 1950's it was unheard of and in Indiana, it was illegal. So, if an inter-racial affair of any type occurred it was always hidden.

Mr. Walker was the town banker. He controlled the town in the 1950's. His house was literally 1 block from the bank, and at times he walked to work, not moving his car. Mr. Walker came home every day to eat lunch because he could. Mr. Walker came home for lunch every day for another reason, Henrietta. Mr. Walker and Henrietta's affair was forbidden but not forced in any way shape or form. Henrietta had the wrong color skin and they both lived in the wrong time in history. Today, Henrietta and Mr. Walker would have been married but not back in the 1950's.

Mrs. Walker had been raised by her mother to control a house but not to please a spouse. She was what most men called frigid. She would perform her duty but like she was a cold salami sandwich on a plate in the refrigerator. She didn't participate, show any signs of passion or provoke Mr. Walker to be intimate with her, day or night. Ms. Henrietta, on the other hand, was taught that at times, you have to use certain skills to survive in this life. Stand up for yourself but if you can use your femininity to get over, use it. What ever worked for you, 'use it' her mother said. Henrietta had a body shaped like a Coca-Cola bottle; which was the term used then and she knew how to move it even in a white uniform. Ms. Henrietta's mother had a very light cream colored, Halle Berry skin complexion and so did Henrietta. In the old black south, this was a sign of the mixed breeding with the slave owner or his assistant on the plantation. The women of Ms. Henrietta's family must have had a knack for attracting white men because the same skin tone was continually passed down from generation to generation. Mr. Walker was nice to Ms. Henrietta. He never forced himself upon her, but each day that she came to work, he watched her and lusted after her body. Jefferson talked to her kindly. He would tease her occasionally when he came home at lunch out of ear shot of Mrs. Walker.

"Henrietta, that uniform crease is pressed so straight, I think I would cut myself if I touched it."

"Thank you, Mr. Walker. Is there something I can get you?" Henrietta said with a low soft voice batting her eyes toward him at the same time. Henrietta knew that Mrs. Walker was not satisfying Mr. Walker. Another day, Henrietta overheard them talking about it through the window while she hung out the laundry. Henrietta also knew exactly how powerful Mr. Walker was in this town and she aimed to capitalize on that power.

Mrs. Walker knew exactly what was going on. She tried to keep Henrietta away from Mr. Walker at lunch time or have her gone, before he came home at the end of the day. She caught him several times looking at her behind and watching her as she walked away. Mary Walker wasn't stupid. She was just bred to be a well-kept lady and not engage in all of that sweaty, sexual activity. Why couldn't they just be civilized, a kiss good night and go to sleep on his side of the bed? Her mother taught her to give them children and they will leave you alone. Things hadn't worked out quite that way for Mary. Jefferson Walker was not trying to have any 'relations' with her so he must be having sex with 'that girl.' Wouldn't his club buddies love to know that he is sleeping with the maid, the 'negro' maid at that? Jefferson was sitting at the breakfast table. They didn't eat much for breakfast so Henrietta wasn't due to the house until 9:00 a.m. and Jefferson was usually gone by then. Mary decided today was the day to approach the subject.

"Jefferson, I want you to stop having sex with that nigger."

"Mary, that is unnecessary. You mean Henrietta? Really? I have needs Mary, what am I supposed to do? Henrietta makes me feel alive and like a real man should feel. You treat me like a business partner. This marriage is a business and not love. You want to impress your bridge club members, come home and do nothing. What about me? You can't have any children. You could at least enjoy some relations with me every now and then." Mary had watched Jefferson come up behind Henrietta while she was hanging the wash on the line outside. He kissed her first and Henrietta giggled slightly. Then Jefferson took her by the hand and led her to his wood shed/garage with a blanket. Mary's heart sank to her feet when she watched this display.

The girl went gladly with her husband. What was she to do? She had to say something to save face and save her marriage.

"Jefferson, you expect me to have 'relations' with you after have you have slept with 'that girl!' I think not. I cannot help it that I can't have children and you know it. The doctors say that there is something wrong with my ovaries. Just because I can't have children doesn't mean that I am going to turn into some roll in the hay whore. I attended Marshall Bennington Charm School for Girls. They had high standards there at that school and instilled that in each of us for our lives," Mary rehearsed.

"Didn't they teach you to have a few low standards when it came to your husband? There had to have been one bad girl at the school."

"Jefferson don't be so crude. We are not animals, we are the highest form of creatures, human beings. I would not have associated with that bad girl at the school any more than I would have associated with any Negroes anywhere on this planet."

"But, getting down and dirty is so much fun. You should try it some time. I will be happy to show you how. Henrietta sure does know how to get down, and she is beautiful, all over."

"Oh Jefferson, you could at least, have the decency to respect me as your wife. I warn you. I could ruin you at the club."

"Don't threaten me, Mary. You try it and you will have to leave town before I am through with you. You will be penniless, naked and alone when I'm through. I have made the money in this house and you didn't. You are an ornament, a fixture on the coffee table and contributing nothing to this house but hot air. Don't you ever forget it!" Jefferson slammed down the newspaper on the kitchen table, grabbed his jacket and gave one last word, "When I come home for lunch today, don't you be here. I am as randy as a rabbit and Henrietta is due here today. I am the man of this house! I am going to have a few rolls in the hay today in a bed that I bought, with a woman who enjoys it and that's that!"

Mary burst into tears and ran out of the room. Just then Henrietta walked into the kitchen after having heard the entire conversation between the Walkers. She didn't let on that she heard anything. When she walked in the kitchen, Jefferson grabbed Henrietta by the arm, turned her so that he could whisper in her ear from behind and said, "I'll be back home for lunch. You be ready for me, you hear."

Henrietta giggled slightly, "I'll be ready, sir."

When Mr. Walker left, Henrietta straightened her uniform and said to herself, 'Well, sir I am going to use what my mama gave me.' From that day forward, Mr. Walker and Henrietta had lunch hours in the spare bedroom. Mrs. Walker left the house to visit family or lunch with friends. It went on for months until it finally happened. Henrietta became pregnant. Mrs. Walker knew that Mr. Walker loved Henrietta and would never let her go, but she knew that Henrietta had to get out of this house. She had stood by and watched her continue to have sex with her husband day after day. But she would not stand or sit by and watch Henrietta's stomach protrude with the seed of her husband growing inside of her. Enough was enough, and she could take no more. Just like the biblical story of Sara and Hagar, Mrs. Walker, said that 'that nigger girl has got to go.'

Henrietta was immediately fired from working at their house, but Henrietta never had to want for anything for her or her child a day in its life. She bore the stigma of birthing a baby out of wedlock to her church members. They asked her repeatedly who the father was but, Henrietta never revealed it. Her church friends tried to convince her to leave town, but Mr. Walker would not let her leave. Henrietta had born him a son. A son was something that he had always wanted. He was not going to let this woman leave with his son and go anyplace. When the child was born, she stopped going to church, but the members found her anyway. She still had to go to the grocery store to provide food for her child.

"What white man raped you girl and gave you that white baby?" Mrs. Greta Wells said to her in the store when the blanket slid back slightly over Jack's head. She named the baby Jack Henry Robinson.

"It's none of your business, Ms. Wells. That is between me and his father," Henrietta snapped back quickly. Even in the 1950s and headed into the 1960s, a woman's body was not her own. If she was caught in the wrong place at the wrong time, she could possibly be taken advantage of. Male relatives were known to rape and molest young women in their own families. Black families didn't tell family business or secrets. The only problem was that Henrietta was in Roberts Junction alone. There was no family to protect her. There was no big mama, father or other siblings to go to the store for her so she could hide at home. She had to bear the public shame alone. Behind closed doors, she enjoyed the love and passion of a man that she could never openly discuss or display. This would have to be enough for her. So, when she was tempted to leave, Jefferson begged her to stay. He created a bank account for Henrietta and whatever money she needed it was there in that account. Mr. Walker bought and furnished a house for her which he visited whenever he pleased. He built a garage so that he could keep his car parked in it when he visited. Henrietta's house was out of the way, but nosy people will drive miles to find out a secret. When peopled asked too many questions, Jefferson would borrow a different car from the local car dealership to drive to her house and leave it outside. Mr. Walker and Henrietta were passionate lovers who would not deny each other any part of each other's bodies. Henrietta had two more babies by Mr. Walker. Another boy and a girl. It was love, but they could never admit it to the world only each other. Henrietta was bound by society's idea of who she should love. Mr. Walker was bound to Mrs. Walker because society said that a real family should be the marriage and children between a white woman and a white man or a black woman and a black man. Neither race should mix and definitely not have children. Over the years, her children knew Mr. Jefferson Walker as Uncle Jefferson. He came to their house to celebrate every child's and Henrietta's birthday. He spent a portion of the day at Henrietta's on every holiday. He would let Mary Walker pick whether he could be with them in the morning, afternoon or late in the evening. It was always Mrs. Walker's choice, but it wasn't her choice at all. She hadn't chosen this life, but she just went along with it. She wished every day that he didn't want to be with Henrietta and her children. But, deep down, she knew that Jefferson would not live with her or himself if he could not take care of Henrietta and their children. She kept their secret. The children never knew that Uncle Jefferson was their father. Henrietta lied and told how each of their fathers had had some mysterious illness or accident that caused their death. The children believed her so much that they hadn't realized that they all looked alike, same skin complexion and body build. The older the children grew they even developed features of Jefferson's family. Each time one of the children pointed it out, Henrietta and Mr. Jefferson would both deny it. That was the difference in children today and then, you obeyed your parents no matter what. If you didn't obey, you paid for it with switches to your behind. Jefferson Walker was the best and nicest white man the Robinson children had ever known. He was their friend, provider and family secret.

Today, Ms. Henrietta's secret was still safe as she sat and put the clothes on hangers. John's secret was safe as he did the heavy lifting of the many bags, boxes and cartons of clothes, appliances and other furnishings to the sorting area. Jamie and Linda's secrets were safe while they sorted, received and prepared them to be labeled and placed on hangers then given to Ms. Henrietta. As employees of Goodwill, they worked together as a team. Everyone knew their job, and if something didn't get done, they all pitched in to get it done. It didn't matter about their secrets as long as they kept working hard and kept their mouths closed. A funny thing about secrets as long as only one person knows the secret, it stays hidden, but when the secret is leaked, it is no longer a secret.

Chapter 5 - Robert

Linda chided herself for even thinking about Robert. Robert was in Linda's thoughts because she had seen and talked to him. She had wondered what he was doing over the years, but seeing him again wasn't good. She was a married woman. Unhappily married, but married none the less. Robert's visit today should mean absolutely nothing to Linda, but it did. It was a pleasant surprise to see Robert, but it awakened something in Linda that she hadn't felt in a long time. The way he spoke her name and inquired about her life was refreshing. She didn't have time to dwell on Robert but, she was thinking about him and that is what scared her the most. What happens when you start to imagine the life that you could have had with someone else? What happens when your past comes back and is standing in your present? She knew that she had to go home and face James and his crazy antics at 6:00. For one day, to have someone pay her some attention was wonderful and horrible all at the same time. She now had a peek into another world of acceptance, decent conversation and a base level of caring by someone that wasn't her husband. As fine as Robert was, intelligent and financially secure, he probably had a girlfriend or at least a steady friend. But Robert said that he wasn't married. Linda had to stop torturing herself with the thought or idea of another life besides this terrible one that she was living. Could there be a way out? Did she want a way out? Maybe not with Robert, but for herself? Did she feel worth it to move on from James and establish her own life, free from abuse, tension and strife? She had stayed because she felt that there was no other choice. Seeing Robert made her think. Her children were growing up and almost ready to leave home. Did she want to stay in that house all alone with just the constant noise of James after Stephen was gone to college?

"Hey girl, are you about ready to wrap up and go home?" Jamie interrupted her thoughts.

"Huh?" Linda was startled by Jamie's question.

"Where were you?" Jamie asked.

"Right here," Linda lied.

"And a thousand miles away all at the same time. Listen, I just want you to know that I was just teasing today. I didn't mean to hurt your feelings or embarrass you," Jamie said.

"Hurt my feelings, no, but embarrass me, yes you did. I forgive you. Remember I am married. This is a very, very small town and I have children in this town. Got it?" Linda asked.

"Got it," Jamie replied.

"Yes, the mighty clock is ticking on the wall and I am about ready to get out of here. I have to decide what's for supper," Linda quickly looked at the clock and realized it was 5:45 p.m. She was about to be off from work. She had to put Robert in the only place he could be, out of her mind for now. This was a Thursday that she would never forget.

Robert couldn't get Linda out of his mind. He knew that she was unhappy at the Goodwill store. He could see it in her eyes. He replayed his visit with her unfaithful husband at the firm. He knew exactly why Linda was unhappy. He also visited James' father, Harold Sanders who was the Managing Partner of the firm. He recalled their conversation as well. Mr. Harold Sanders, Sr. expressed to Robert that he would be retiring soon and was looking for someone to turn his firm over to.

Robert asked Harold, "So what about one of your sons taking over the firm? I saw James downstairs and know that he is not licensed to practice, but can he stay on and run the office?" Robert was sitting across from Mr. Sanders' small cedar table in his office. This table had 6 chairs around it. Adjacent to the office was a larger conference room with a huge cedar table with 20 chairs around it.

"James can't run his own house," The elder Sanders leaned forward and explained, "James can't be trusted. I only keep him on because he is my son. His mother and I spoiled him as a child. He had learning problems in school, and he couldn't keep up academically with his brothers. He also got hurt and couldn't recover physically to play football on the college level. He has had little correction throughout his whole life so James just runs wild and does whatever he wants to do. He doesn't know that I know that he is sleeping with every woman in this firm that will let him. He pretends that I don't know, but I have called him into my office and warned him about his behavior. I have also told him that if one of these girls gets pregnant, he is gone. I don't care if he is my son. James disrespects his wife, children and family by his behavior. I don't know what to do with the boy, but he has to have a livelihood somewhere. If he didn't work here, I don't know what he would do. He can sure get a woman to lift up her skirts. I guess he could sell cars or furniture. His wife works at the Goodwill just to get out of the house away from him. He treats her poorly and if she had the nerve, I believe she would leave his ass. I can't blame her if she did. What do you see in the future of your firm?" Robert explained to Mr. Harold Sanders, Sr. what he envisioned with his firm and why he returned to Roberts Junction.

James was a cheater and was cheating on Linda right now. Robert knew what cheating did to a person and their future. Robert had cheated on Linda in high school with Janice. She didn't deserve that type of treatment. Robert remembered how she looked, what she had on and how red her eyes were from crying that awful day. Linda broke up with him all those years ago because Janice Brooks was now pregnant. He couldn't blame Linda. He hadn't meant for that to happen, but he was drunk and Janice took advantage. He remembered the conversation verbatim. "So, Janice is pregnant?" Linda asked through tears.

"Yes," Robert answered calmly.

"Let me get this straight. You didn't take me to the Homecoming Dance because you wanted to go with Janice?" The hurt, disgust and embarrassment were evident in Linda's face.

"No, I didn't want to go with Janice, but you weren't accepting my calls. You wouldn't talk to me in the hallway because you were mad at me. I always wanted to take you to the dance, but you wouldn't call me back!" Robert exclaimed.

"I know that was my fault. I listened to Becky who told me that I should play hard to get," Linda said.

"You listened to Becky who hasn't had a boyfriend all school year. Play hard to get? Becky should be happy with whatever she can get. I explained that I didn't call you back on last Tuesday because practice was late!"

"Becky said she saw you talking to Janice after football and cheerleading practice when she was coming home from debate team practice. She said that she saw Janice touch your arm."

"Becky also forgot to tell you that I pulled my arm back and told her not to touch me."

"No, she did not."

"Sounds like jealousy to me. Becky is jealous of you and you let her tell you only one part of the truth to break us up. She doesn't have a boyfriend and doesn't want you to have one as well."

"But now it is too late. Janice is pregnant. Are you going to marry her?"

"Marry her? I am not ready to marry anyone? I only love and want to marry one person, you."

"Well, you blew that one."

Robert watched as Linda walked out of his life and to a life with James a few months later. He really thought that James cared about Linda. James and Robert always were in competition. They competed with each other on the football field and that's what being with Linda meant to James. It was a way to compete and win over Robert. He prayed that one day that he would get another chance to win back the love that he threw away for one night with Janice. Linda never knew that he and Janice never slept together again after that Homecoming night. He was only in connection with Janice for the sake of his child, period. He took care of his responsibility and now that responsibility was a lovely young woman that would one day take care of him.

Robert checked into the local, brand-new Holiday Inn Express on the highway for the night. Tomorrow would be Friday and he would head back to Indianapolis after he had met with the leasing manager about the office space for his firm. He made a quick call to his office manager, David Noles, in Indianapolis.

"Hello Robert. How are things in Roberts Junction?"

"In a word, interesting."

"What do you mean?"

"Well, everything is fine with the building location and I am going to finalize things in the morning with the leasing officer, but it is the people in this town. They really haven't changed."

"Got in on a little small-town gossip I take it."

"Yes, among other things."

"What's her name?"

"What makes you say that?"

"Just something in your voice."

"Well, Mr. Nosy, it is an old girlfriend of mine from high school that I saw today. I had some time and remembered that I needed some shirts for the boys at the Marion County from Boys to Men Project. I went into the local Goodwill and there she was. She didn't really recognize me at first, but I knew her right off. I am so much taller than her that she didn't look up into my face directly. Her eyes landed around my chest until I made her recognize me."

"So, what is the problem?"

"She is married to the town jerk, and I am just concerned about her."

"Concerned only?"

"Yep, right now all I can be is concerned because she is committed to the jerk."

"You know, Robert, there are a thousand women in Indianapolis you could be with and would love to be with you in a heartbeat. You are concerned about a woman in a Southern Indiana town like Roberts Junction. What is so particular about this woman?"

"I was young and messed up years ago. I think that I could have been married to her right now, but I let one night of Hennessy, boobs and ass get in the way of true love. I am paying for it. I need to make it right. I feel like there is just some unfinished business between us. Also, she doesn't deserve the life that she is living whether she chose it or it chose her. She deserves much better. Surprisingly enough her husband is the office manager of the firm I visited today," Robert explained.

"Be careful. Remember she is a grown ass woman and not a child that you have to rescue. If she is married to the man, she stood before a judge or a preacher and said yes of her own freewill," David added.

"You are right. But I think that her free will was pushed and coerced a little by my actions." There was a sadness in Robert's voice just thinking about what he could have or should have done back then.

"Maybe. Is there anything else you need from me?" David could hear the tone in his boss' voice and he knew to move forward with the conversation.

"I just need you to be standing by in the office with cell phone handy between 10:30 and 11:30. I want to get this lease wrapped up before I leave town. I am tired from the drive and all of the information I found out today. I am headed to bed in a few minutes and hope to sleep late awakening just prior to my meeting. I am driving back tomorrow afternoon. I probably won't come to the office, but will be in the office on Monday morning early."

"I will be waiting by the phone. Be careful on your return to Indianapolis. By the way, the weather man says that there is some snow that is supposed to start moving in around 3:00 p.m. tomorrow."

"Thank you, 'Old Mother Hubbard', for giving me the heads up. I will be safe," Robert said.

"Don't blame me if you get stuck on the side of the road. You know how Indiana snow storms just show up quickly dumping a lot of snow, and then there you are off the side of the road in the ditch waiting for hours for a tow truck." Robert chuckled at David's account.

"See you Monday. Goodnight."

"Goodnight." Robert pressed 'end' on his phone and picked up the remote to turn on the television. All three ESPN channels were on this television, but he really wasn't paying attention. It was background noise that filled the room. Robert set the sleep timer for 45 minutes on the television. Sleep came quickly. He hadn't needed 45 minutes because Linda entered his dreams from the start.

Chapter 6 - James

James got started on his weekend a little early. He was on the couch in front of the television working on his third beer of the six pack. Linda pulled into the driveway and saw James' car and knew that it was going to be a rough night. She liked getting home before him. She preferred getting herself prepared for him to come home rather than walking in and responding to whatever mood he was in. She noticed the Guinness packaging in the trash can in the garage. Linda didn't drink at all. She saw enough of what drinking could do to a person and family as a child. She wanted no parts of it. Fresh, cold, sparkling ginger ale was as bubbly as she got with her drinks.

James had purchased a one floor ranch style home with a basement. They had lived in this home for about 15 years. The first floor had a living room, dining room that connected to the kitchen, there was their bedroom and another smaller bedroom that served as an office/man cave or meeting place when friends came over. The boys' bedroom was located in the basement and away from everyone. There was no exit or walk out from the basement, but it was great privacy for them as well as a shelter during tornado warnings and bad storms. As soon as Linda opened the door from the garage and put her keys on the counter, it started.

"Where you been?" James snapped, not taking his eyes off of the television relaxed in his brown lounge chair.

"Work."

"It's almost 6:30, where did you go?"

"Once we wrapped up the work at the store, I went to the gas station to fill up before I leave for Bloomington after work tomorrow for the game. That's all."

"You didn't call so I didn't know."

'I didn't call?' That was all that was going through Linda's mind. How James could fix his mouth to say, 'you didn't call' Linda did not know. When did James ever call her to tell her he was going to be late? When did he call to say he was going to a dinner party with the lawyers from the firm or stopping to get a beer and watch the game at the local pub? James never ceased to amaze Linda. She recalled all of the dinners she found in the refrigerator that she had put there, the night before, expecting that James heat up the plate in the microwave when he came home. 'I didn't call.'

"Sorry. You hungry?" Linda didn't know what else to say. Linda wasn't sorry, but James was so calm right now she didn't want to get him started.

"No, not really. These beers are doing it for me right now. I am fine." James was not in the mood for arguing or getting mad at Linda tonight. Linda was a good woman and he should treat and talk to her better, but he just couldn't. There were too many other choices out there for him to just settle down with just one-woman night after night. Even at the thought, James blew it out of his mind. He was James Sanders. What that meant exactly in his forties, he still didn't know. A person of his age should be more mature and learn to appreciate what he had with Linda, but he wouldn't and couldn't. He had always gotten out of messes since the 3rd grade when he and his buddies had stolen the chocolate candy from the storage closet at Roberts Junction Elementary. He had been the mastermind of the wicked plot to steal the candy, sell it and then get the money for himself. His father was the town lawyer. Their family had plenty of money, clout and power in this town, but that was no fun for James. James craved excitement. His teachers warned him all of the time to 'stay focus on what is important, academics and not just fun or recess.' Mrs. Weathers in class 103, God rest her soul, knew that James Sanders was a part of stealing that chocolate candy out of the storage closet because he had left her room to go to the bathroom. The problem was she couldn't prove it. Those were the days before hidden, security cameras were allowed in the school. It was Mrs. Weathers' word again his. He won that time. By his high school years, there were security cameras. He still got caught stealing money from the athletic director's office which was located in the old gym isolated from the main building. The athletic director had just counted the money from the athletic bake sale and concession stand during lunch period but, left it in his desk because gym class was about to start. The athletic director knew that he was going to turn in the money to the bookkeeper, after he finished his class. James spoke to the athletic director when he came in and went to work out in the weight room. James saw the money on the desk and knew that he had to have it. He didn't need the money, he just wanted it. The videotape did not lie. It was James seen on the screen taking the money out of the drawer and putting it in his pocket. James' dad got him off because it was the big game on that Friday between Roberts Junction High and rivals, Scottsburg High from one county over. The athletic director was as competitive as they come. He didn't want to lose. He wanted to win the game on Friday and knew that they would win with James. So as usual, the authorities at school made an exception for James and the vicious cycle of privilege continued.

Just like high school, he had gotten caught today by Robert Matthews. He should be embarrassed, but he was not. He should be trying to cover his tracks, but he was not. He was his same bastard self. Robert Matthews could use his knowledge of the incident against him, but he knew that his dad had his back on whatever happened in his life. Harold Sanders, Sr. had always saved James time and time again.

"Is Stephen home?"

"No, he stayed over his friend Brian's house tonight because they are studying for a big test or doing some big project together. He's leaving for camp with that church you hooked him up with, after school tomorrow." Linda knew that they were going to be home alone and anything was subject to be said or done.

"Yes. Well, I will just fix something just in case you get hungry later," Linda's voice trailed off quietly as she was moving swiftly around the kitchen.

"I said, I am fine!" James' voice was loud and with emphasis on the fine. He could have gone much farther with that statement but didn't have the energy for that tonight. Linda held her breath for what was about to be said next. "Linda, just let me sit here, get drunk and enjoy the game."

"Okay," Linda mumbled under her breath because she didn't have much air to say much of anything else. She realized that she had been holding her breath. It was a good thing because if she said more, he might hear her and get louder or say something more. She couldn't risk it. She knew that the alcohol was talking and James didn't need any help with the verbal abuse. She covered the plate of chicken, rice and green beans with plastic wrap, and it went into the refrigerator like normal. The Thursday Night football game was about to start so that kept James' attention for a while. She ate her food on a paper plate quickly and went to the bedroom to begin packing. As she put her clothes in bag, she thought, 'What if I packed all of my clothes and left for good? What would he do then?' Where would I go or where would I live? I don't want to leave my house, but I have got to get out of this situation here. James hadn't talked to Linda the whole time the game was on or while she was eating. He didn't share any of his day or his thoughts but treated her like a servant. It was like Linda had no feelings, no ideas, no thoughts but just a servant that never seemed to please the one she was serving. Nothing she did was good enough. Nothing she said was good enough. He controlled everything in the house except her money. He did let her keep her money from the Goodwill. He talked down and demeaned her about the amount of her checks as much as possible. The old saying is that 'if you don't spend it, even pennies mount up.' Wouldn't James love to know how much money Linda really had? The one thing that James did do well was make sure that she had grocery money each week and pay the household bills. Other than that, she bought her own clothes, put gas in her car and anything else she wanted to buy, she bought it. Was she really living? No, she was surviving. Linda's work at the Goodwill and her home life didn't collide. They couldn't collide because Linda did not want anybody to have a peek into the dysfunction that she lived with every day. This wasn't 1940 but, 2014. She could divorce James and move on with her life but what about her children? If she looked closely, her children were practically grown men. Even at the ages of 20 and 17, they would be devastated if she left their father. What Linda really wanted most of all at this point in her life, was true love.

Everything was ready for the weekend. Linda had just showered, changed into night clothes and was under the covers to bring on sleep. Just then she was flipped over quickly and James entered her as soon as she was flipped.

James loved to take her from behind, because her face was down and she could not fight. It never was a fair fight. James always seemed to get the best of the situation. He used to coerce her into have sex. At others times, he would make her cry and pretend she had done something to make him mad prior to sex. Now, it was rape. He treated her just like his old football days. This wasn't a football game. She wasn't another football player with the same strength and capacity to be able to combat this attack. She was supposed to be his wife. Fortunately, she hadn't put on any powder or drying lotion tonight, so she was still kind of moist from her shower. As she got older, she was getting more and more dry which made her bleed from his multi-intrusions.

"Please stop." Only those two words could be uttered from muffled sounds coming out of Linda when she turned her head to the side on the pillow. She knew that he wouldn't stop even if she begged and pleaded. The tears flowed hot on the pillow beneath her head. These were the new tears that were just piling on top of the last group of tears that she shed from the last time he invaded her. She was a woman not a country, battle ship or other enemy that he was trying to conquer and enslave. She was not his enemy, but supposed to be his wife.

Unbeknownst to Linda, James had already had sex earlier that day with the firm's receptionist. James always had an insatiable sexual appetite. James was selfish. It didn't matter about the other person. It didn't matter that Linda was tired from her job today. It didn't matter to James how often, when and with whom. He just wanted what he wanted when he wanted it. The person's feelings, and especially Linda's feelings, never mattered, it was all about him. The flip move that James used to flip Linda for sex was at one time fun. It was foreplay. He used to say things like, 'Here I come. I want you babe so much and thankful that you are in my life.' He used to kiss her madly all over prior to doing anything. They both had thought it was fun because he would tease that she couldn't gain weight because she would mess up his greatest sex move. They both laughed then, but neither were laughing now. Linda wanted to think that back then they were really in love. Linda realized now that they weren't in love. She had seen from her parents what real love looks like. Real love grows, in spite of the good and bad times. The admiration, commitment and caring for one another continues to grow and grow. Real love grows. Whatever James and Linda had, whether it was infatuation, like or just an attachment, because they had two babies, was long gone.

"Humph," James uttered more like a grunt than a word in Linda's right ear. James exited Linda's body on cue by the ESPN music heard from the living room. The half time show of the game had ended and so had the half time misery show ended in the 'James Sanders' bedroom.' James rolled off of Linda and stumbled back down the hallway in only a t-shirt and nothing on the bottom to finish watching the game. Linda continued to muffle the sounds of her tears in the pillow before going to the bathroom and taking a second shower. She kept telling herself, 'I don't deserve this. I am worth more than this. I must somehow get out of this situation.' Linda knew that if these words were ever going to be reality, major changes would have to take place in her life. Telling yourself these words is good and a start, but she knew that eventually action would have to take place. Linda took a second shower, put on new pajamas, changed her pillow case and prayed for sleep.

Sleep came slow and was interrupted by a dream. In the dream, Robert looked good enough for the runway and a magazine cover. In the dream, he had on a dark blue blazer with gold buttons, a crisp white shirt and a pair of khaki pants as they were headed into a house dining room. Somehow Linda looked down and there was a bulge of arousal in Robert's pants which showed just how much desire he had for her even before the meal. Robert assisted Linda with her seat while motioning for her to look at the table decorations with candles and flowers, that were especially for her, on the dinner table. A blazing fire was in the fireplace and its light shown in the background. A musician was playing soft music on the violin in the background. Linda could not tell what song was playing but could feel the rhythm of the song by the body movement of the musician. The setting looked beautiful and a prelude for a night of passion. In her dream, she wanted to come closer, but dared not, because she saw James over in the corner yelling at her that 'you are mine forever.' If this dream was any indication, Linda knew that the nightmare that she had been living for twenty years would continue.

Chapter 7 – The Meeting

Linda woke up at 5:30 a.m. and left the house before James woke up. She packed the car quickly and treated herself to breakfast at the local *Waffle House*. It was game day, Friday, payday and escaping day for Linda.

James woke up at 8:00 a.m. and realized that Linda was gone. He rolled over and found his cell phone and speed dialed the number.

"Hello."

"Hey, how are you this morning?"

"Fine."

"Are you free tonight?"

"Why, what did you have in mind?"

"Well, a steak dinner, some wine and a whole lot of me."

"In that order?"

"We can have that in any order or repeat the action as many times that you want," James chuckled and the woman on the other line giggled slightly.

"I'll be ready, Jimmy, with as many jimmies as we are going to need to get this party started right."

"I like the sound of that. About 7:00 p.m. alright with you?"

"Anytime, anywhere and anyway is alright with me."

"That's my girl. See you tonight," James got a hard on just listening to her voice on the other line. When he hung up the phone, he ran to the shower to have his own release while imagining all of the things that they were going to do to each other tonight. Linda was gone until Sunday. Stephen was going on a camping trip to Brown County with the local church group. Perfect. With the house empty, James thought he would bring his latest fling back to the house. He was tired of spending money on hotels and motels out of the county. He had a house, a bed and a private garage so he would bring her here. He was a man and he wanted to do what men do with a woman who they really want to be with. 'All kinds of things in every room in this house,' James thought as he spilled his seed on the floor of the shower one more time.

Helen Black, John's mother, woke up at 7:00 a.m. and called out from her bedroom, "John you are coming straight home from work today, right?" Helen was buttoning the last two buttons of her housecoat and putting her feet in her house shoes to go to the kitchen and say goodbye to John before he left for work.

"Yes, Mom. I am working until they close, and then I will be home." John was putting his coffee cup and empty bowl from his cereal in the sink. Their small 3-bedroom house was so small that you could be in any room and you could hear someone's conversation all over the house. John never would have any privacy as long as he stayed in this small house. The house was only large enough for the two of them to live.

"I left the list on the table of everything that I need you to pick up from the grocery on your way home."

"Mom, can't I get this on Saturday when I am off work?"

"You know how I want you to have everything for dinner for the entire weekend by Friday. I really don't want you going to the grocery on Saturday because I might need you to help in the house with some other things. You are such a good son. I really don't know what I would do without you."

"Have you ever thought about what you would do if something happened to me?" John finally got bold enough to ask.

"Don't say that!" Helen grabbed her chest like she was having a heart attack. "You promised you wouldn't leave me. You promised."

"I know I promised, but what about my life? What about me? Have you ever thought about me?"

"Don't I treat you good John? Don't I fix good meals and treat you good? Have you met someone?"

"How can I meet someone when I am here all of the time? I am either at work or home, that's it. I don't go out. I don't go on dates. I will be fifty years old soon! I want a life too you know."

"These women mean you no good out there. I am your mother. I gave birth to you. I am really the only one that loves you for real."

"Mother, you do love me, but not in the same way that a woman can. I have had a few times that I have met a woman at a hotel to meet my needs. But I couldn't spend the night holding her in my arms because you would call and ask where I was and what I was doing. I was making love and having a great time. That's what I was doing!"

"Don't you disrespect me, John Black! I am still your mother."

"That is the point, you will always be my mother, but not my girlfriend or my wife! I want a wife and my own life! I am going to have that kind of life before I die. I am just letting you know that now."

"You would rather watch me sit here, dwindle up and die to have that life. If you are not here to take care of me that's going to happen, I will just die."

"Mom, we all are going to die sometime." Helen burst into tears. She grabbed a tissue and covered her mouth like John had just slapped her.

"Oh, Johnny you have hurt your mother today so badly. I don't want you to go anywhere else. I want you to be right here with me, close by. I am your mother. Your father left me to die." John usually gave in and stopped the conversation cold, but this time he kept going. He realized that he had to stop longing for that life, but start building that life one step at a time. The first brick in that life would have to be making his mother understand her role in his life.

"Stop right there. I have heard that story one hundred times and not ready to hear it tonight. Know this, I will always make sure that you have what you need. You are not in a wheel chair, bed bound or unable to take care of your basic needs. I realize that I am all that you have right here in

Roberts Junction, but I need and want this for myself. I will promise you one thing. I will not date a woman who does not understand that I have to see about my mother. Who knows, she may have to take care of her parents too. At our age, it is understandable and must be taken into consideration when dating anyone. But I will not subject a woman to even dating me and meeting you unless YOU understand that you are not going to be calling twenty times a day for nonsense either. Once I secure your needs, unless it is truly an emergency, it can wait until the next day. I will not be running, jumping and coming over here for every little thing that could have waited until another day and time."

"You would move out?" Helen let out another round of fresh tears.

"Yes, I would move out. My place is only being rented right now. I have not sold it. I know that having two women in the same house is a disaster. You would have an opinion on every pot holder to the type of cleanser to what food should be served and on which night. I wouldn't put a woman that I loved through that. A fresh start, new relationship, a new lady, our house and a new life."

"It's going to take me some time to get used to it. I think you should wait at least a year before you start this process of finding someone and all."

"A year! I will not wait or waste another second. That is it and I am done talking about it! No, I do not have someone I am seeing just yet, but I will." In John's mind, that was a promise. His mother was just going to have to understand and deal with the reality that her baby was finally standing on his own two feet to be a man and take action.

"I can't believe that you would do this," Helen's voice was breaking up again heading towards a new round of tears.

"I can't believe that you would do this to me either. You say you love me, but want to hold me back like I am a small child. Just because you don't want to move forward in your life doesn't mean that I don't want to move forward with mine. I am going to the store to get what's on the list prior to going to work. I have changed my mind. I am not coming home straight after work today. I don't know what I am going to do, but it won't be coming straight home. Don't fix me any dinner tonight. Only take care of yourself. I am going out, where to I don't know and don't care. I just know I won't be straight home from work today," John snatched the list off of the table, went out the back door and let the door slam.

Helen sat down at the table and went into another round of new tears. 'My life is over again,' she thought. 'What to do?'

Helen thought about it and cried even hard because she could still hear John's father's voice many years ago saying, "Helen Black, you haven't been a wife to me in years. I have begged and pleaded with you to come out places with me. I have asked you to join other couples, get a babysitter and go out with me so that we can leave this house, but you refuse. I am done begging and pleading with you. We don't need to live our life together. I have met someone and I am leaving you." John Black, Sr. uttered those awful words almost 20 years ago, the bags were fully packed and waiting at the back door. John Sr. picked up those bags and walked out that same door. John Jr. was at school, and when he came home, his dad was gone for good.

Helen's ability to keep her husband were no more successful than trying to keep her daddy home from leaving her mama even more years before. All of the men in her life left her. Her granddaddy left her grandmother. Her daddy left her mom and her husband left her. It was a vicious cycle that was going to continue if she didn't stop John, Jr. from leaving her too. Helen could still hear herself say, "No, John, you can't leave me. I had you a son, John, Jr. wasn't that enough? I am not like you, adventuresome and outgoing. I am a home body. I just want you to come home, have dinner, read the paper, watch a little television and we go to bed until the next day. You can go have fun with John Jr. I don't like going out. I just like being at home." In spite of her words, John Sr. turned and the door slammed against the house as it closed. That sound brought on a headache that wouldn't quit and closed up her heart to only her son.

John Jr. felt bad about how he had talked to his mother, but it couldn't be helped. She had pushed him too far and he must finally take a stand. John pulled into the handicapped parking space at the local grocery store and he retrieved a basket at the entrance. He got out his list from his pocket and began to map out his strategy. There was milk, apples, meat and cheese from the deli as well as brownie mix, toilet paper and towel paper were also needed. Just as he was about to take off for the produce section, he bumped his cart into another cart. Looking up, his eyes met the face of a lovely woman with a small child in the cart.

"Excuse me," John said immediately after the slight hesitation in the movement of his cart.

"Excuse me. I am sorry. I wasn't looking where I was going."

"Neither was I. I have my mind on this list."

"Uh oh, Gammy I think you hit somebody," the little boy with the bluest eyes and curly blonde hair called out in a high pitch sing song voice like a nursery rhyme. John and the woman laughed nervously both looking at the little boy in the cart.

"Yes, Bradley, Gammy hit this man's cart, but I said sorry."

"Good, Gammy said sorry. Now Bradley says sorry for Gammy hitting your cart," the little boy said.

"That is fine. Bradley, is it?" John smiled as he looked at the woman's face again to get her response to the question.

"Yes."

"Bradley thank you very much. You are both forgiven." John said as he awkwardly put two hands on his cart and began moving along the short zig zag aisles in the produce department. When he arrived at the deli counter, there she was again.

"There he is Gammy." Bradley looked about 3 years old with a big smile that would light up any one's life.

"Yes, Bradley, there he is."

"Hello again Bradley. What are you and Gammy getting from the deli?" John asked as he looked down at Bradley.

"Ham. I like ham. My Gammy likes ham too."

"Really? What else does your Gammy like?" John was hoping to entertain Bradley while his gammy continue to look over the items in the deli case. John didn't know what gammy meant. He didn't know whether she was his mother or grandmother. She looked very young to be a grandmother, but who knew these days. John wasn't very good at pickup lines but he wanted to know if she was married, single or in a relationship.

"She likes cookies, milk and turkey too."

"I like cookies, milk and turkey too. Thanks for the information, Bradley."

"Bradley, that's enough talking for now. I think that you are getting on this nice man's nerves. Sometimes mine too," she mouthed to John over Bradley's head. John laughed out loud. She liked how he laughed. "Well, we have everything we need from here. Bye," the lady said as she pushed her cart away from John and to the store checkout line.

"Bye," Bradley said and waved back to John as they moved further away from him.

"Bye," was all that John could say back. The young woman behind the counter asked if she could help John with something in the deli. John gave her his order and when he turned around, they were out of sight. Every aisle that John passed he looked for Bradley and his Gammy, but no luck. Oh well, another time he would have to try to get in the store early and maybe he could possibly see her again. What was he thinking? She could be involved with somebody, have a steady boyfriend or worse, she could be married! He couldn't get his hopes up based on this random incident. John was spreading his wings this morning and he wanted to fly. He had waited long enough avoiding eye contact with women around the city so they wouldn't notice him. He was ready to be noticed, acknowledged and more importantly, loved. When John returned home, the kitchen was cleaned and no sign of his mom.

"Mom!" There was no answer. John assumed that his mom wasn't answering because she was still mad at him. John put away the groceries and decided to check on her one more time. So, he called out again, "Mom!" He moved closer to her bedroom and knocked on the door. When she didn't answer, he opened the door and found her on the floor. She was laying completely still and not making a sound to even call out to him. John ran to her side and rolled her over. Her eyes and mouth were both closed. He almost tried to sit her up but remembered that she might have broken something and he shouldn't try to move her. He slowly reclined her gently back on the floor and grabbed her phone on the night stand and called 911. Helen heard John dialing the number and frantically trying to tell the 911 operator what was going on with her.

"It's my mother. I went to the grocery and when I came back home, my mother was lying on the floor.

Helen quietly called out John's name, very weak at first, "John? Is that you?"

"Hold on ma'am." John still had the phone in his hand when he came around to the other side of the bed to check on his mom who had called out to him. "Yeah, mom it's me. Are you alright?"

"I don't know what happened."

"Just lay there, I am calling the ambulance."

"John, hang up that phone. We don't have money for no ambulance. Just help me up and get me back in the bed so you can go to work." Helen reached out her arms for John to pick her up like a baby.

John told the operator, "My mom seems to be coming around. She doesn't want to go to the hospital, and I am going to do whatever she tells me to do." The operator tried to convince John to bring his mom to the hospital because she could have suffered from a broken bone or a sprained ligament that he couldn't recognize right away. "I understand but, if she doesn't want to go. I can't make her. Thank you so much. Goodbye." John hung up the phone and returned to his mom.

"Mom, I am not going to work today. I am staying home with you all day, today."

"Are you sure? I will be fine, just get me back in the bed. Can you go get me a cold compress in the bathroom?" When John left the room to put cold water on the towel, his mother smiled slightly. She had won this round. It was true that she had been laying down after he left for the grocery store, but that was to give her time to plan her strategy. She could hear his truck when he turned it on to the gravel driveway. He hadn't even realized that this little episode totally changed his plans for the day and evening. Helen was going to teach him about going against the wishes of his mother. He was going to pay and never leave her. She hadn't fought hard enough to keep his father, but she'd be damned if he would leave too.

Steve opened the back doors of the store and said, "John won't be in today because his mother fell. He is staying home with her today. He called me at home so I came in a little early since you guys are going to be short staffed today."

"Do we need to get them anything?" Jamie asked Steve seemingly really concerned about John and his mother. Steve just hunched his shoulders and left the back room. One thing Steve only wanted to know enough to get through the daily shifts. If it wasn't his business or critical to running the Goodwill, he wasn't involved in it.

"No, Jamie you don't need to do nothing. John is a grown ass man and can handle his mother. He should call an ambulance if there is any real trouble," Ms. Henrietta answered for Steve.

"Jamie, you are always ready to meddle in something you know nothing about. John has warned you about that too many times," Linda interjected. "Have you ever met John's mother?"

"No."

"So how would you even know the first thing to do for her or John?"

"I don't know. I just thought that I would offer to help. As far as meddling, I really wasn't meddling this time. I am really concerned. I really only like to meddle with you, Linda. Ha!" Jamie laughed out loud.

"Laugh all you want to, but stay out of my business and it will be better for everybody concerned," Linda demanded.

"Alright. You never know," Jamie conceded.

"I know that we have a lot of work to do today so stop all of that jawing and get to work," Linda added with an attitude. "Jamie let's get the rest of these shirts on that rack out there. Remember I am leaving at 2:00 p.m. today for William's game in Bloomington."

"Okay, but it was these same shirts that got you in a little trouble on yesterday," Jamie giggled.

"Shut up, Jamie, and let's go."

"You both need to keep working because we are short-handed seeing that John is not coming in today," Ms. Henrietta added.

The day continued to run smooth and Linda was counting down the minutes until she left town and her problems. With only 30 minutes left for Linda's day, who walks in, but Robert. Steve came to the back again and said, "Linda, you have a visitor."

"For me?"

"Yes. He said, Linda, and that's you," Steve hunched his shoulders again and left the storage room.

"I wonder if something has happened to Steve or William?" Linda said as she left the storage room. Nosy Jamie was right behind her and stopped short of the door hitting her in the face. Jamie was used to catching the door so she could peek and see what was going on, on the main floor.

"Ms. Henrietta, come quick and look. It is Linda's high school sweetheart again."

"Stop, Jamie, already."

"I know, but he is so handsome and tall."

"I learned a long time ago to stop longing for things that you just can't have or even shouldn't have. Don't go lusting after something that isn't or won't ever be mine," Ms. Henrietta said.

"Ms. Henrietta, I don't know when, but I am going to get mine," Jamie stated.

"Okay, baby, make sure that it's really yours and not somebody else's," said Ms. Henrietta.

Jamie whipped her head around quickly and said, "Ms. Henrietta, you think that about me?"

"Child temptation is hard and it makes you do things that you don't really intend to do," Ms. Henrietta said.

"Not me," Jamie said under her breath.

Linda headed toward the front of the store and looked up to see the back of Robert's head. Linda stopped in her tracks straightening her top and jeans before she reached him. She quickly ran her hand in her hair to secure her ponytail. Why she did this she will never know. Robert was so fine that any real woman, happily married or not, would just have to take notice. Linda didn't know what was wrong with the Indianapolis women. Had they suddenly gone blind not to see this wonderful, gorgeous, intelligent man walking around free in that big city? It was magnetic. Why did he come back to Roberts Junction? He could have had another law office anywhere, but he picked Roberts Junction. Why had he come into the Goodwill? He couldn't get shirts in Walmart?

"Hello," Robert heard her footsteps, turned and looked down at the top of Linda's head because she wouldn't look up at him. She looked up briefly and her face was just as he had dreamed.

"Hello again. How are you?" Linda looked down again to avoid Robert's eyes. He was trying hard to look directly into hers.

"I am fine. I was about to leave town, and I wanted to get a few more shirts before I left. I also wanted to stop by and tell you goodbye."

"Oh, okay about those shirts," Linda ignored the comment about stopping by especially to tell her goodbye. She thought if she ignored it, she wouldn't have to acknowledge it. "Those shirts are still in the same place they were yesterday," Linda waved her hand in the direction of the shirt rack. She tried to walk away, but her feet weren't cooperating.

Robert was watching her very nervous actions and wondered if she had been thinking about him as much as he had been thinking about her.

Linda continued, "Steve is up front, and he will take care of you. I am leaving in a few minutes." Linda was mad at herself for saying that out loud. It wasn't any of Robert's business where she was going or what she was doing. She should have been calling or checking in with her husband,

James, but he could care less about what Linda was doing as long as the house was clean.

"Are you headed home? Are you okay?" Robert asked concerned.

"No, I am going to Bloomington for the game. My oldest son William plays football. It's the IU Purdue game. I go to all of the home games." Internally, Linda reprimanded herself for saying that so freely to Robert.

"Really, so you are a football mom? You still like football from high school, huh?" Robert asked.

"I have always loved football, but I love my son more and want to support him."

"James is going too?"

"No, he is working."

"James is working on game day? That is too bad." Robert was so tall over Linda that she didn't see that slight smile come over his face. Robert thought, 'That dog was at it again. Well, he was no slouch and could play that game too.'

"Linda, excuse me really quick, I need to make a call."

"No problem, I am going to head back to the break room and gather my things to leave." Linda thought that would get Robert to leave. That didn't happen.

"I'll wait for you."

Linda couldn't believe it, 'wait for me.' This was not a date why was Robert waiting for her? She went to the back quickly and announced to everyone, "I am headed out and see you guys on Monday."

"Heading out with Mr. tall, dark and handsome?" Jamie teased with a whisper.

"No, I am headed to my car and driving to Bloomington alone," Linda mouthed through very tight lips.

"Be careful Linda. Jamie and I will take care of things until you get back on Monday," Ms. Henrietta called after her.

"Thanks Ms. Henrietta. I am convinced that you are the only sane one in the place. This girl right here is going to drive me to..." Linda pointed directly to Jamie.

"Ignore that girl. It is already 5 minutes after 2. Get there before the traffic backs up too far getting onto campus with all them gaters or whatever you call 'em."

"Tailgaters, Ms. Henrietta," Jamie added while giving a quick chuckle at the misplaced words.

"Whatever, just be careful. Do you have a heavy coat?" Ms. Henrietta inquired.

"No, I am fine with this hoodie and another jacket on top."

"Young folks. It is November and a storm can rise up with no notice. By the way, where is your hat, scarf and gloves? Did you forget how cold the football field is 'chile?"

Linda chuckled under her breath. "Ms. Henrietta, I love you too, but I already have a mother." She really did love Ms. Henrietta. She always cared about her when other people didn't seem to give a damn whether Linda lived or died.

"Alright don't come to me when you are sick and can't come to work. I told you so. At least, zip up the hoodie thing."

While Linda went to the back, Robert had an idea to treat Linda special. Robert opened his phone and made a quick call. "Hey, George, do you still have those box seats at the Indiana Stadium?"

"Yeah Robert, always for you. You coming up?"

"Yeah, I am going to have a friend with me."

"A young lady is accompanying you finally? I can't wait to tell Kelli."

"Don't tell Kelli nothing. That will scare the hell out of my friend. It is not a date but a friend from high school. Her son plays for the team."

"Okay, I won't tell Kelli, but you know she is bold. If she sees you with her, she is going to inquire about you, her, the status of your relationship including the name of your first born." Robert started to laugh.

"Yeah, I know, but I will have to cross that bridge when I come to it. I am leaving Roberts Junction now and should be there by 4:00 p.m."

"That's pushing it, because we start tailgating at 4:30 p.m. The game starts at 7:30 p.m."

"Okay, I will call you when I get off I-65."

"Cool."

Linda was headed toward Robert with her IU t-shirt, hoodie and athletic department jacket. "You ready?"

"For what?" Linda said as she was digging for her keys and double checking that she still had her mind and her purse.

"To leave?"

"Yes."

"Where is your car?" They headed out the side door of the store to the back parking lot.

"Out back. Why?"

"I am about to leave and thought that I would follow you up."

"Why?"

"Why not? Which car is yours and what is your cell number?"

"My car is that blue Jeep Cherokee and I don't have a cell phone."

"Who doesn't have a cell phone?"

"A person that no one calls."

"What does that mean?"

"Just what I said. No one calls me."

"What about your sons? How do they call you if something goes wrong?"

"They both have a cell phone. They call their dad on his phone or call me at the store. Nothing abnormal usually happens. We get our plans scheduled in the morning and everything usually runs smooth."

"Wow, I don't know how I would live without my phone."

"Well, that's the difference between you and me. You are important and have important business to take care of, so you need a cell phone."

"Wait one minute," Robert stopped Linda in the middle of the parking lot and with both of his hands on her shoulders, turned her toward him, "You have associated being important with having a cell phone. I don't like that because the drug dealer on the street has a cell phone. Let's get one thing straight. You are important whether you have a cell phone or not. On the other hand, it is dangerous not to have a cell phone on the road. I am not going to talk about your husband, but he is an idiot not to have given you a cell phone earlier. So, wait right here until I bring my car around to you. I am driving a white Lincoln." Linda was almost tempted to run to her car and drive off. Robert could feel that she wanted to run, but he turned quickly and called her bluff.

"Linda, I am serious, don't get in your car and drive off. I am a member of the court. I will call in a favor," Robert smiled which caused Linda to stop and slightly smile back, "Look at that. I think I might have made you smile."

"Come on, Robert. It's getting late, and I want to get out of here."

Robert loved the sound of his name coming from her lips. "Wow, you finally said my name. Give me just a minute to pull around and meet you."

Linda got in her Jeep to at least wait for Robert pull his car around. It was a beautiful, very large, white Navigator. She had seen them on TV, but never in person and certainly had not ridden in one. Robert stepped out of the truck again. Linda watched him walk toward her Jeep and she thought, 'he's beautiful.' He knocked on her window and she rolled it down.

"Here is an extra cell phone, and here is my business card. Call the number on the card if you want anything."

"How do I use it?"

"Don't worry, I am going to call you in a minute. To answer it, just press this button right here."

Robert walked back to his car, got in and dialed the number. 'James is a damn selfish fool,' Robert thought and said some other not so nice things about James under his breath while getting back in the car. The phone rang, Linda pressed the button and put the phone to her ear.

"Hello," Linda said after she pushed the answer button.

"Okay, great you have learned lesson number one, how to answer the phone," Robert said as Linda giggled.

"A giggle out of Linda. I am a freakin' genius," Robert added.

"Okay, freakin' genius. What is lesson number two?" Linda asked.

"Lesson number two is how to put the phone on speaker so you won't get a ticket while we talk and drive. Do you see that green button at the bottom of the phone?"

"Yes."

"Press it," Linda pressed the button and could still hear Robert's voice. "Can you still hear me?"

"Yes," Linda said slowly, but excited that she was learning something new.

"Great. Put the phone on the seat, and let's get going. No more lessons on the cell phone until later." Linda and Robert continued this light banter all of the way up I-65. Robert took the lead all of the way to Bloomington which was fine with Linda. She knew that traffic was going to be a bear and he seemed to know where he was going. The traffic increased once they got closer to the Bloomington exit. She usually didn't see William until after the game but, because Robert was in tow, she didn't know how things would work out tonight.

"Linda, just follow close behind me. There is no need for two cars trying to park so we can stop by my friend's place and leave your car before heading over to the stadium."

"Will that be alright? He won't have my car towed, will he?"

"No, he is my friend and won't tow your car. I will call him and let him know. Don't be nervous, you do remember how to answer the phone?" Robert wasn't quite ready to tell her that it was his house and not a friend's.

"Yes."

"Okay, I am going to hang up, call him and let him know. Then I am going to call you back. Okay?" Robert wanted Linda to be as comfortable with him as possible. This was an adventure for both of them.

"Okay."

Robert made the quick call to George and called Linda back.

"Hello."

"Hello. I did it!" Linda was hesitant at first, but got excited when she answered the call and everything worked.

"Yes, you got me back on the phone and put me on speaker at the same time. Yippee!"

"Don't make fun of me."

"I am not making fun of you. I am genuinely happy that you were able to work the phone. I am still pissed that James hasn't bought you a phone sooner. Okay, that's the last time I am going to fuss about that tonight."

"One day I will have my own phone. Don't you worry," Linda said emphatically.

"You can rest assured that one day that you will have your own cell phone," Robert pulled into a private driveway in a very plush neighborhood where a lot of professors at Indiana University lived. Each lawn was manicured to perfection. The sign at the entrance read, 'Indiana Meadows Private Drive.' Linda tried not to stare while enjoying the beautiful neighborhood, but it was hard. Robert pulled his Navigator into a large two-story house with four posts in the front, plenty of shrubs and beautiful pathway lighting leading to the front door. Robert put his hand on the visor and touched a button and the garage door opened. Robert got out and walked to her truck. He told Linda to drive in, bring the cell phone with her and lock her doors. Linda agreed and thought, 'Robert must be really close to these people to have their garage door opener which literally leads to the inside of their house.'

Linda walked out to Robert's car. Robert opened the passenger door of his truck and settled her in his SUV. She suddenly felt under dressed. If she had known this was going to happen, she would have worn a little better pair of jeans or her new boots and not these old sneakers. It was too late now. Robert was dressed in jeans and a shirt so she guessed that was alright.

"You didn't have to get out to let me in. I am quite capable."

"I can tell that you haven't had the treatment in a while young lady."

"The treatment?" Linda asked.

"Yes, for you to ask what the treatment is, it's been far too long. I am the king of the treatment."

"Wow. Yes, I guess it has been that long. Oh mighty king, what is the treatment?" Linda asked.

"The treatment is when a real man is trying to impress a real lady and he does, buys or says whatever to please her."

"Oh my, that's the treatment," Linda said and thought to herself, 'You are the king of the treatment? I have never had the treatment. I have had bad treatment but never this type of treatment.'

"Excuse me, did you say something?" Linda didn't realize that Robert could read her thoughts. Why was he asking her had she said something? She hadn't said anything out loud, but her brain was thinking very loud.

"No, I didn't say anything. But I should at least say thank you. You have saved me $15 to park tonight."

"You are welcome." Robert thought to himself, 'she's real practical with her money too. She has probably had to be practical with everything since that bastard hasn't even provided her with a damn phone. Who does that? I won't.' Robert was glad that Linda couldn't read his thoughts.

They continued toward the stadium. Linda was able to really take in the sights of this college town since Robert was driving. The temperature had been in the lower 50's all day, but now that the sun was going down, there was a sudden drop in temperature. Cool temperatures, football and hot chocolate or hot coffee all seemed to go together along with the excitement and anticipation of a great football game. People were walking with extra blankets, hats, gloves, scarves and extra socks. People had started partying early because the conversations were getting louder and louder. This was going to be a great night for football. Linda remembered coming to the games back in high school with her ear muffs, sweat pants or leggings that were added to her cheerleading outfit to cheer for the Roberts Junction Ravens. Linda's father and mother would go to the games with her. Her mom worked the concession stand, and her dad watched the game from the stands. She always asked him, "You ready dad?" He always answered, "Yes, princess, I am ready 'cause I got my long johns under these jeans, so I am really ready." Linda's dad used to wear long johns in the winter and especially to the games. She thought of her dad now with a smile. He loved football so much. He would have loved to come to the games with her to see his grandson play. 'I hate cancer,' Linda thought. Daddy would have also been wondering why James wouldn't take off from work to spend more time with his family too. Linda put the thoughts about James behind her for now. She would deal with those thoughts another day.

Normally, the college games were played on Saturday at noon, but this was a special league game that could only be scheduled on Friday night. The town was filled to capacity with people up and down the street, eating dinner, drinking beers and meeting up with friends.

Robert pulled into the VIP/Faculty Parking Lot and parked behind a huge smoking grill, plenty of chairs and a spread of food that could feed an army.

"Good evening, Mr. Matthews."

"Good evening, Ryan. How are you?"

"Fine sir. It is good to see you again. Do you want me to park your car for you?"

"It's good to see you too. No, Ryan I am going to park my own car this evening, but thanks so much. How are classes?"

"Fine sir. I should graduate in December and be in one of your classes by next spring."

"Great. Congratulations. I look forward to it."

Linda's mind was racing. She turned her face to the window so that Ryan wouldn't notice her. He didn't say anything so she felt that she was in the clear for now. Linda thought, 'What did Robert really do? She thought he was a lawyer in Indianapolis. What did he do in Bloomington? Teach? Mentor? Who were these people that they were getting closer and closer to in this very large vehicle of his? Lord, what have I done? I should have left the Goodwill alone and when I was supposed to.' Linda almost lost it. Robert stopped the car and turned to Linda. He could see that she was fidgeting in her seat and possible anxious.

"Now before you freak out, let me explain. Please look at me Linda." Linda raised her head to look into Robert's eyes and saw real concern. She really wanted to cry because she hadn't seen that much concern for her in years. First the 'treatment' and now this conversation.

"Okay, please start explaining quickly before I can't breathe."

"Take a deep breath before I start," Robert watched Linda take a long deep breath in and out. "I am a lawyer and have a firm in Indianapolis. I also teach here at the law school in Bloomington. I know most of the students who are interested in law, enrolled in law school currently or recently graduated from law school. I work as a recruiter in addition to a professor and my practice. I mentor youth in Indianapolis just like I said when I came into the store to buy those shirts. Besides my daughter and a few investments, I have had nothing or no one to spend my money on. So, I bought a house here in Bloomington for me and my friends to stay on game day or to spend the night when I didn't feel like driving back to Indianapolis. I am in Roberts Junction because I have some people in Louisville who want me to represent them. So, I decided to kill two birds with one stone by opening an office in Roberts Junction. It is near home, and I can give back to where I grew up. My parents died years ago, as you know, and I have no one but my daughter, Jennifer. I believe that my dad would have been proud. He was a farmer and unable to go to college, but did all he could to help, prepare and support me through school. I am not now dating or have I ever dated much since you in high school. I have a standing invitation to tailgate in the faculty area with some law professors, attorney friends of mine and other colleagues on campus. I have told my friend, George, that I was bringing someone with me, but that we are strictly friends and that is it. I have only brought Jennifer with me to the games and no one else. They are excited that I am bringing someone so don't take offense if they try to categorize us as dating. I told George that you were strictly a friend from high school that has a son that plays on the IU football team. I know that you are married. I wouldn't want anything to jeopardize that. Do you trust and believe me?"

"I really think that I should have come alone. Ryan didn't notice me with you which is good. I can't see William until after the game anyway, and James is not coming. I guess this will be fine. I gave in because you were coming this way anyway. I must confess that I am overwhelmed by it all. I don't know how I will explain everything to James, but I will survive."

"If you feel too uncomfortable, let me know, and we will leave," Robert said, pleading with his eyes for Linda to stay.

"I will be fine. I am sure that your friends are nice and will be considerate. I also know that the law business is a small one in Indiana and people may talk. It looks really awkward me being here with you especially without James."

"I understand."

"I am going to the game. I promised. It is too late to turn around, go back, get my car and return to campus. Let's go."

"Great." They both got out of the car and headed toward the big red tent. Robert introduced her to everyone as a high school friend from his home town who just happened to be coming to the game to see her son play. He didn't explain too much, but wanted no one to assume anything about their relationship. Robert made no effort to touch or get too close to Linda to appear that there was anything inappropriate going on between them. Everything inside of him wanted to betray that, but he was committed to her being as comfortable, in a very uncomfortable situation, as possible. George's wife wasn't convinced, and she watched them closely the whole time they were outside. This was out of character for Robert to bring anybody besides Jennifer to the games. Oh well, she would have to keep her eyes on this one even though she could clearly see the wedding band on her finger, it didn't mean anything.

"Are you okay, Linda?" Robert said checking on her while still outside.

"Yes, I am fine, but I need to go in and say hi to William before the game."

"Okay. I have box seats, and you can join us to get out of the cold if you want."

"Wow, that is nice, but I need to go to the bleachers first and say hello. That is what I normally do at the game. I, at least, want to keep that same routine. I will try to join you in the box after half time." Linda knew that she was rambling because she was nervous and couldn't help it.

"Do you go to dinner with your son after the game?"

"Yes, we sometimes go out to eat unless he has plans with his friends. I have a reservation at the Fairfield Inn this weekend, so I can go and come as I please."

"You have the cell phone, so we can communicate via phone as soon as you know your plans."

"Okay. Thank you so much, Robert, for everything."

"Let me get that blanket in the back for you to have in the bleachers." Robert walked to the car and left Linda sitting at the tent.

"Hello," a voice came from behind Linda. Linda turned around into the face of Kelli who was George's wife.

"Hello to you too." Kelli extended her hand out to Linda.

"I am Kelli, George's wife. Your name is Linda, is it?"

"Yes, it is."

"So how long have you known Robert?"

"Most of my life."

"That is a long time. Did you go to school at IU or you just here for the game?"

"No, I am here for the game. My son plays on the football team and I came to watch him play."

"Where is his father; he not with you?"

"No, he had to work tonight."

"So sorry to hear that. Well, it was a pleasure meeting you and hopefully we will see each other later." Kelli wondered how any real father could miss this once in a lifetime home game on a Friday night. Maybe he wasn't a football fan? Maybe he had a second shift job that wouldn't allow him to take off? Or, maybe she was not really with his son's father anymore, and they were separated. Kelli's mind was racing trying to figure why this woman was really here. A game, yes, but was she here with Robert only for the game?

All Linda could say in return was, "It's good to meet you too." She was ready to leave this area and go into the stands with all of the other thousands of people, away from the spotlight of this lady, Kelli and her group of friends. They were looking at her strangely and Kelli asked too many questions for her taste.

Robert returned with the blanket, and not only handed it to the Linda, but preceded to put the blanket around Linda as she gathered her things to walk into the stadium. "Here you go."

"Thank you. Ms. Henrietta was fussing at me earlier because I didn't have a heavier coat, gloves or scarf with me for the game. She was right. I should have come prepared because it has turned cold and smells like snow. I love to look at snow but don't like to drive in it."

"You'll be fine." Robert thought, 'if I have anything do with it you will be in my house looking out at the snow and not driving in it.'

Robert watched as Linda walked away from him, headed inside the stadium. Robert hoped that he would see her later, and they leave together just like they came in together.

Kelli approached Robert as Linda walked away, "So, how close friends are you to Linda, Robert?"

"Excuse me?" Robert turned and asked Kelli with an attitude.

"Well, it is so unlike you to bring someone besides Jennifer to the game so I was curious how close friends are you to Linda?"

"Can you keep a secret?"

"Yes."

"So can I," Robert said as he walked back to his chair to finish his beer. Kelli just stood there for a moment and then walked away herself. She knew that she has crossed the line with Robert, but he told her all that she wanted to know by not telling her.

There was nothing like a real college football stadium. The seats, the field, the band and the people. Everything was crowded and loud. The anticipation was building between both schools' fans, the cheerleaders and the supporting bands. The people were getting themselves settled because the game was about to begin.

"Hey William!" Linda called out to her son from the gated area just behind the IU home bench. Even above the noise of the thousands of people, William could hear his mom's voice. 'She made it,' he thought.

"Hi Mom!" William was getting more handsome every day as Linda watched him walk toward the fence. He looked like his dad but had none of his attributes.

"How are you?"

"I am fine. Where is Dad?"

"He is not coming, because he had to work."

"Okay," William said sadly.

"William what is the plan for after the game?"

"If we win, I am staying on campus. If we lose, I am headed home to hang out with Becky."

"Becky? I thought you guys broke up over summer?"

"We did, but we have been talking again. It's her birthday this weekend. I wanted to go home to surprise her and celebrate with her and her family. She has been to several games so I wanted to go home and support her."

"No problem. That is wonderful son. I will wait for the outcome of the game and then I'll decide if I stay or go home early tomorrow. Please be careful out there today, and I love you Will."

"I love you too, Mom."

This was a good game, and surprisingly, Indiana was winning 14 to 7 at the half, as the team ran off of the field. Linda gathered up her things and headed to wait in the long line with the other thousands of women. When she came out of the restroom, she saw the sign to box seating. She decided to call Robert.

"Hello."

"Okay, you win. I have had enough of this cold weather, and I am going to come sit on the inside. I am standing here looking at the sign that says box seats, but which number are you seated?"

"Great. The number is twelve. I'll be standing in the hallway waiting for you." Robert was excited that Linda would be joining him in the sports box. He remembered, more than 25 years ago, on their first date the excitement of seeing and being with Linda. He had to calm down and remind himself that she's married.

Linda and Robert enjoyed the comfort of the box for the remainder of the game. The other guests did not talk to or bother Linda or Robert during the game. Unfortunately, Indiana lost the game by a field goal, with only one minute left in the game. Linda knew that William would be heading home to be with Becky for her birthday. It still smelled like snow, but the snow had not started so Linda hoped that William would get home before it started. Everybody was making plans on what to do after the game. William didn't see his mom in the stands, so he figured that she was headed back to the hotel. He was headed to the dorms to meet Ryan so they could head home. Ryan texted William and said, 'I am at the dorms ready to go when you are.'

William texted back, 'give me 10 minutes. Quick shower and be right there. Already packed.'

Ryan returned his text, 'cool.'

Robert knew that Linda didn't want to be with the group any longer so he navigated their way through the crowd until they got to his car.

"Are you hungry?" Robert asked.

"I am starved."

"Did you get anything at the concession stand at the game?"

"No, they charge too much for that stuff."

"You have a point."

"Why don't I whip up some pasta, make a salad and open a bottle of wine."

"I need to get my stuff and head to the hotel."

"Without eating? The King of the Treatment does not let a lady leave him without eating."

"Well, I guess I could get you to buy me a free meal after all of the humiliation with your friends."

"Humiliation? What humiliation?"

"Maybe that is the wrong word. How about being unprepared for that many people on that level to meet at one time."

"Okay I will give you that."

"So, you can cook?"

"Can I cook? Of course, I can cook. How do you think I have lived alone, not married, still alive and not cook? I would starve. Oh, I get it, you doubt my skills?"

"Umm, I don't know nothing about your cooking skills. We only ate hot dogs from the concession stand at the games when we were together. You never cooked for me. Back then, a hot dog or hamburger stand was a big deal."

"Hell yeah, it was a big deal. You were a big deal to me."

"Flattery won't get you anything until I taste the pasta."

"Oh my, I think I have awakened your humor too. I'm on a roll. Only problem is with this traffic, it looks like you are going to be hungry for a little while longer."

"No problem. I know that it will be worth it, or you will pay."

"What did you have in mind?"

"Look at you with your mind all down in the gutter."

"I am a guy. Every guy has his mind in the gutter when there is a woman around." They both laughed. It took them about an hour to get 5 miles to Robert's house.

When they pulled up, the third car garage door opened and he pulled the car in to a complete stop. Robert turned to Linda. "I have a confession."

"What's that?"

"This is not my friend's home. This is my home. I didn't mean to lie, but I really didn't want to overwhelm you," Robert said.

"Really? I thought you said you lived in Indianapolis?" Linda asked.

"I do, but I teach so much here I bought a home here."

"Wow. You don't owe me an explanation," Linda said.

"Yes, I do. I am sorry. Will you still let me cook for you?" Robert asked.

Just then Linda's stomach growled really loud. "I guess my stomach answered for me." They both laughed. Robert hoped that he hadn't lost Linda's trust. Robert remembered his mom said that he would still be lying even if he said nothing. Trust was too hard to come by and so easy to lose. Linda still had Robert's cell phone and left her things in her car. She was even more nervous being alone with Robert in his house. Linda told herself, 'He hasn't really lied, but didn't tell the whole truth either. He hadn't been inappropriate and she was very hungry.' Linda realized that she didn't have a real reason not to trust him so she stayed.

Robert told Linda to wait in the car while he got the garage light. He came back to the car and gave her more of 'the treatment.' With only her purse in tow, she followed Robert to the garage door which opened to a very spacious house and directly into the kitchen. From the kitchen, it was a tri-level house and an open floor plan from the first floor to the second. The kitchen, to the living room, the hallway leading to the back bedrooms were easily seen from one vantage point. There was a fire place on the lower level which had an exit out onto a deck. Just like in her dream. Robert enjoyed warm colors, oak furniture and comfortable large chairs and couches because he was so tall. He spent days and nights here with friends, his daughter or alone working. There was a theater room, a grand office with a large conference room for planning and meetings. He brought another woman here once. She didn't quite understand the nature of their relationship because she started offering her own decorating ideas. It was the one time that Robert tried to open up to someone new and he quickly realized that she wasn't the one. Robert wanted to pinch himself knowing that he now had the opportunity to share it with the one woman he had loved all of his life. Linda. He messed up once, but if given another chance, he would move heaven and earth to be with her. Walking into that Goodwill changed his day and hopefully, his life.

Robert turned on some soft music, settled her on the couch in the den and told her to make herself at home.

"Do you need any help in there?"

"Nope, I am fine. Do you need to call anybody or check in?"

"I would like to call William because he is on the road. I don't want your number to pop up on his caller ID."

"It won't. I have a private number on my home phone. Pick up that phone on the end table and call out. No number, name or anything else will show up. This is my private get away and I don't give out this number to anybody. Go ahead," Linda dialed William's number easily and there was only one ring.

"Hello," William answered because no young person is ever without their phone.

"Hey, William, it's Mom."

"Hey, Mom, are you okay?"

"Yes, I am fine. I didn't see you come back out onto the field to say goodbye."

"No, I looked for you in the stands, and you weren't there."

"I had gone to the bathroom upstairs. Sorry you guys lost the game."

"Thanks, Mom. That's life, you win some and some time you lose. We did our best."

"Yes, you did. Where are you?"

"We are about 45 miles away from home. Where are you?"

"I have reservations at the Fairfield Inn on the highway." Linda didn't tell William where she was exactly, because she didn't want to lie. She didn't lie because she still had reservations at the hotel, but she just wasn't there right at that moment. Linda realized fully in that moment why Robert didn't tell her about his home. Some things need to be shared in small increments.

"Okay, be careful, and I will see you on Sunday. I am riding with Ryan. He texted me and we met up at the dorms. It was too crowded and I wanted to get out of town as soon as we could. We are planning to go by Becky's house to take her and Alicia to the late, late movie.

"Are you going home to sleep?"

"No, I will probably stay at Ryan's so we can leave when we need to tomorrow or Sunday. Love you and have a great night." Ryan Parker was a senior at IU and William was just a sophomore, but they had been friends in high school even though they were two years apart. Ryan had a younger brother, Jason, who was also a friend and classmate of Stephen.

"You two just be careful. I love you."

"Love you too, Mom." Linda hung up the phone and gently wiped her eye. 'How did I get here?' she thought. 'My children are grown, but my husband doesn't act responsible to them or to me. What am I going to do?'

"Everything okay?" Robert asked softly while watching her at the counter in the kitchen.

"Yes. It's just real sad about how things turn out sometimes."

"What do you mean?"

"Nothing." Linda didn't want to get emotional, but she felt that she had to let it out sometime. If not now, when? There was silence and Linda was staring straight ahead at nothing. Robert quickly turned the sauce on low, the pasta water off and put the salads in the refrigerator. He walked over to the couch where Linda was sitting and sat down beside her not too close to crowd her.

"Tell me. Everything is on low on the stove, and I really want to know." Linda began to cry while trying to gather her thoughts and explain.

"This is not the life that I planned on living. I thought that James was really serious about being with me and creating a family together. A lot of what I am feeling is tied to my sons getting older and moving on with their lives. The so called 'empty nest syndrome' is real, but I don't know what our relationship has become. I know what kind of man James has become, and that is no example to my sons."

"What do you mean by that?"

"James is crazy. He is mean, inconsiderate, and irresponsible and doesn't love me at all. He has been a provider for the house and bills, but that is all. He hasn't been there for me as a husband or for the boys as an example of a father. I don't really know why I even said all of that, but you are probably the only person beside Ms. Henrietta at the store who has sat long enough to really listen or even wanted to listen to what I have had to say in twenty years. You know?"

"Yes, I know, and I am so sorry for any part that I played in that," Robert said calmly.

"I haven't thought about that in years," Linda said.

"I have thought about it every day of my life," Robert said.

"That's incredible," Linda said as she looked into his very handsome face. She held his gaze for only a second before she turned away. Linda thought, 'I can't keep looking into his eyes. That's trouble.' Where that came from, she didn't have a clue.

Robert wanted to reach out and touch her, but he resisted. He wanted to let her get it out before he offered. He hadn't been around Linda in twenty years, so what touch would be appropriate that would be comforting without seeming invasive? He decided to let it come naturally.

Linda continued, "On the other hand, I don't know what I am waiting on to live the life I was designed to live. You know?"

Robert wanted to scream out, 'Nothing! You are staying here with me and never going back to that bastard again.' He knew that he couldn't make that decision for Linda. She had to come to that conclusion on her own.

With all of the reserve he had in his body, Robert replied, "That's your decision to make and not mine. I will say this, I want you to be safe and happy. I don't believe that any woman should be with a man that doesn't make her deliriously happy. I know that men are jerks, make mistakes and embarrass their women at times. In the end, at the core of every man should be someone who he loves passionately, protects fiercely and provides abundantly. That's it."

Linda was wiping her eyes with her hands. Robert reached up, and with only his thumb, wiped a tear from her right eye while she caught the other one from her left.

"How did you get so smart about relationships, Mr. Matthews?"

"By being a total failure at relationships. Remember I am the guy who was dating the love of my life, but has a one-night stand with the high school slut and gets her pregnant. I gain a lifetime of a beautiful daughter, but not in a loving relationship with her mama. How dumb is that? My daughter is wonderful. I am blessed to have her in my life, but the relationship doesn't make a great role model for her either. I have been very honest about it all to my daughter."

"Go back. Rewind. I was the love of your life?"

"Yes, you still are."

"Wow," was the only word that Linda could think to say at that moment.

"That's the truth. Do you mind if I give you a hug?"

"No. I think I need one."

Robert opened his arms out wide, and Linda went into his arms gladly. She hadn't been hugged by masculine, strong, safe arms since her daddy died. Robert held her for a long time and just let her cry it all out in his shirt. Fortunately, they were sitting so their height difference did not matter. Robert cupped her head with one hand and slowly rubbed her back with the other while she cried. Linda felt so good in his arms. Robert made her feel safe and she had only reconnected with him after a day. Robert seemed to be interested in what she had to say, feel and need. Linda realized that she wasn't free to enjoy Robert like this. She needed to, in Jamie's words, "pull up" or she was about to crash onto his lap. She also realized that Robert's shirt was wet from her tears.

"Oh goodness, look at your shirt," Robert knew his shirt was wet. He could feel it, but it didn't matter. He wanted to be the balm that soothed the hurt away from Linda if only for tonight. He put one hand through her curly hair. He remembered pulling her curly ponytail to tease her back in school.

"You act like I can't get another shirt, girl."

"I know, but I have unloaded all of my emotional garbage on you."

"That's what friends are for. You feel better?" Robert asked and Linda could only nod her head, "That is great, but I think I heard your stomach growl again even louder."

"Yep, me too. That's embarrassing."

"Don't be embarrassed. I am shirking on my cooking and feeding you duties."

"I think I will faint from hunger soon."

"Well, let's fix that."

"Can I help?"

"Yep, there are dishes in that cabinet over there so set the table and I will re-heat the water for the pasta really quick and we will get this food thing done and relax." Robert and Linda enjoyed a great meal with light conversation filled with laughter and no more tears. They cleaned up the kitchen, took their wine to the lower-level living area and Robert started a fire. The dry wood took to the match quickly. He put on some soft music and sat down next to Linda on the very comfy sectional couch. He normally was sitting here watching the news or a game, but tonight he was watching Linda.

"The fire is beautiful," The filling, delicious dinner and wine was relaxing Linda now, "I need to finish this glass of wine and head to the hotel. What time is it?"

"It's eleven thirty." Robert looked at the lighted clock on the credenza.

"I had better hurry."

"Why don't you just stay here? I have five bedrooms and one can have your name on it. I really don't think you should drive in your very relaxed condition. Stay."

"Are you trying to say I am tipsy?" Linda asked. She hadn't been tipsy since the bottles of champagne that she and James shared on their honeymoon.

"No, just really relaxed. Stay." Robert looked into Linda's eyes and she smiled. She hadn't been this relaxed around anyone in years. She stayed tense all of the time at home because she didn't know when James' anger would erupt.

"Seriously, I need to go because the hotel will charge my credit card for the night's stay even if I don't show up."

"We can solve that right now." Robert reached in his wallet and pulled out $150 and put it in Linda's hand. He gently held on to her hand and the money so she couldn't throw it back at him. "That should take care of the room, tax and any other charges. Stay. Please." Linda looked into Robert's eyes. His soft plea was tugging at her heart. She knew it was wrong and she should leave. Two wrongs don't make one right, but she could get lost in his eyes. She didn't know if it was the wine or what, but she suddenly wanted touch his hair.

"I'll stay. I shouldn't, but I'll stay," Linda heard herself say. Just then Robert's Bose Stereo read his mind and started playing Brandy singing, '*Have you ever loved somebody so much it makes you cry.*'

"Can I have this dance?" Robert asked while still holding Linda's gaze.

"Oh, my goodness. I haven't danced in years and I'm not very good," Linda giggled slightly.

"You don't need to be a good dancer just hold on to me," Robert said as he grabbed the remote and turned up the volume. Linda put her glass on the coffee table on a coaster and joined Robert in the middle of room. He took the remote and turned up the volume.

Her head gently rested on Robert's chest where it seemed to belong. Her hands rested on his shoulders and his hands met in a circle at her waist. He pulled her closer and rested his head on the top of head just like so many high school homecoming dances years before. Robert stood six foot four and Linda stood only five foot eight, but she fit perfectly in his arms. This was heaven to Robert and a dream come true. They rocked to the beat of the song and got lost in each other's arms. Linda breathed in Robert's essence, his cologne and his care. She wanted to remember this and, in her mind, carry a piece of him home with her. Robert lifted his head from Linda's and she lifted her face up toward him. Like the pull of a magnet, their faces were drawn to each other. They came together for a kiss that would not be stopped or denied. Torn apart by circumstance but reunited by this kiss. Their mouths opened and their tongues did the dance that set off rockets and fireworks in their heads and bodies.

"I am sorry," Robert said first. Holding Linda slightly, but steady so she wouldn't try to dart out of his arms.

"I'm not," Linda said surprising herself in between short heavy breaths.

"I will do whatever you want to do."

"Do you really want to know what I want?"

"Please tell me," He thought he would explode right there on the spot. His chest was rising and falling with each choppy breath. He had waited so long for this moment.

"Make love to me."

Robert didn't think twice. He leaned down and picked Linda up in his strong arms in one swift motion cradling her like a baby. She was light as a feather and right now, his baby. He didn't want to waste time and thought once about making love on the couch. It was big enough for the both of them and soft enough for all night but she deserved better. They resumed getting reacquainted via hands, mouths and tongues. He was starved for her love, her touch and her kiss. He could find his way through his house in the dark, with a blind fold on and no hands. That was what it was going to take to make it to his bedroom. Even with his eyes closed, he held Linda as close as possible so she wouldn't bump into anything. Linda resisted no more and put both hands into Robert's hair. He groaned loudly in her mouth. He climbed the short steps to the next landing and then another few steps and down the hall to the master bedroom. It had a big four poster bed like something in a palace. Robert laid Linda on the bed like she was a porcelain doll.

"I want to make tonight beautiful for you. Don't move a muscle," Robert stood up and rolled up his sleeves, "I will be right back."

He went into the bathroom, ran a warm bath, found a bottle of Jennifer's bubble bath and some candles. Linda was laying quietly on the bed. She couldn't believe herself, but she really didn't want to run or try to hide. Surprisingly, her mind was not racing, wondering or scared about anything. She was for once living in the moment. All those years of horrible was about to be erased with this one night of wonderful. How she would find the strength to leave Robert she didn't know or care at this moment. Robert returned and picked her up again and carried her to the bathroom. He had lit candles around a huge, oval shaped, bubble filled tub.

"Oh, Robert," Linda whispered in disbelief knowing that this was all prepared for her. Robert was standing behind Linda and not able to see her face, but the pleasure and whisper in her voice said it all. She wanted to break down and cry right then, but two fat tears rolled down instead.

He turned to face her and said, "I know that I haven't seen you in twenty years. I know I hurt you deeply so many years ago but right here, right now, I want you to trust me," Linda nodded her head slowly and he continued, "I know I don't deserve your trust, but I sure want to earn it. If you are uncomfortable with anything, just say stop and I will stop immediately. Okay?" Linda nodded her head again.

He bent down and kissed the tears away from her face. He first removed the ponytail holder from her head and let her hair fall. He began removing her clothes one layer at a time. He folded each piece of clothing creating a neat pile on the adjacent chair next to the bath tub. He kissed her mouth and any part of her body that was exposed after he removed that piece of clothing. Linda thought she would melt from the gentleness of his kisses. She was so wet and she hadn't gotten in the bathtub yet. This wetness was coming from inside of her. She had been buying products to help her problem, but really the wrong man was her problem. She was so overwhelmed by Robert's care and time that he took with her she cried again. He did everything. She already had had multiple orgasms, and he hadn't even come into her yet. He lifted Linda again and placed her in the bathtub. He washed and lavished attention to every part of her body exploring every layer of her through the bubbles. His hands and mouth used interchangeably to have her crying out, moaning and scream in ecstasy. He massaged every muscle of her body including extra care to her feet because he knew that she stood all day. He was wet himself from Linda writing from the pleasure and the water splashing on him. He didn't mind. He wanted to please her. He left her only briefly to find shampoo to wash her hair and two t-shirts. He had pleasured her so long that the water went cold twice. After some time, He dried her with a warm towel he retrieved from the dryer and dressed her in one of his t-shirts. He picked her up again and gently laid her in the bed and under the covers. She was fast asleep. He remained in his wet clothes and sat down in a nearby chair. Tears slowly slipped down his face because Linda Harris was actually sleeping in his bed. Not in a million years would he have guessed. He had prayed a long time and his prayers were finally answered. He didn't know exactly how long he had been sitting there, but he decided to remove his wet clothes and step under the hot stream of water.

Linda woke up immediately at the sound of the powerful spray of water. She was a mother first and any sudden noise would wake her up. She oriented herself to the room and realized that she was still at Robert's house. He was in the shower. She used to surprise James in the shower, but that hadn't happened in years. She wanted to see if she still had it. She removed Robert's t-shirt she was wearing and slipped in the bathroom unbeknownst to him and opened the shower door to his surprise.

"Hello," Robert turned at the sound of her voice.

"Hello to you too." He had seen her naked already. Linda presenting herself to him again on her own made him even more aroused than he could have imagined.

"My mother always said when someone does something nice for you to always know how to say thank you. I believe it's my turn to say thank you."

"You don't have to because it was my pleasure."

"One pleasure deserves another and another." This time Linda explored Robert's body first with her hands and then her mouth. He spread his arms and legs wide to let her have full access to him. She could hold back no longer and guided him inside her body for the ride of their lives on the bench inside of the shower. Their bodies were in total sync and timing. The in and out, thrusting deeper and deeper with moans and cries for more from two people who wanted each other desperately never gets old or loses its thrill. This love making session was twenty years past due. This moment was important because they didn't know when they would get another. It was amazing how being with Robert gave her the power to be someone new. It was a new Linda. He made her want to express herself sexually and verbally without ridicule. No put downs, demeaning words or laughter directed at her that was not funny. He never forced himself on her but allowed her to do to his body what she wanted. She went down on her knees and took him in her mouth a little at a time. He was much bigger and longer than James. He made no moves to touch her head, which she hated, or guide her in any way. She must have done something right, because he screamed when he came. The sound of pleasure and satisfaction was all that Linda wanted to hear. When she stood, he kissed her one more time which brought another round of pleasure on the shower bench.

Chapter 8 - Grace

Back in Roberts Junction, John was content to wait on his mom hand and foot all day on Friday. He fluffed her pillows behind her back and put one under her feet. He brought her water when she was thirsty. Brought her meals to her bed side and even walked her to the bathroom each and every time that she went. He discretely stood outside of the bathroom, but wanted to be close by just in case something happened, and she fell again. Deep down he wanted to go to the grocery for any excuse to see if that young woman would be there with Bradley.

The next day John peeked into his mother's room to find her asleep, dead to the world. She was tired, and he didn't wake her up, but hurried to the store. As he went into the store, he got a basket and just started walking up and down the aisles. When he got to the frozen food section, he thought he recognized the coat of the young woman that he met on Friday morning. He moved his basket toward her and said, "Well, hello again, Bradley's mom."

She turned quickly and started to laugh oh so slightly and said, "Well, hello to you as well. I am not Bradley's mom. I am Bradley's grandmother"

"You are a grandmother?"

"Yes, I am."

"Wow, when your grandson called you Gammy, I figured that's what he meant, but you looked young enough to be his mother and not his grandmother."

"Thank you," She blushed.

"You are quite welcome. My name is John by the way."

"My name is Grace."

"What a lovely name for a beautiful lady," Grace blushed again.

"Thank you again."

"Where is our friend Bradley?"

"It is Saturday so his mother is off from work and he is home with her. After seeing me here for the second morning in a row, you can tell that I like to shop early in the morning because it is quiet and without Bradley, it is even quieter." John and Grace both laughed unexpectedly.

"He is just a very talkative and active little boy."

"Try living with him and you would know that active is not the word."

"Well, that is good to know that he is what we call all boy," John said with a smile.

"To say the least. What are you here to buy?" Grace asked.

"I thought I might get some cinnamon rolls for my mother. She got ill yesterday and I thought I would give her a treat."

"That's nice. Do you live with your mother?" John remembered that it is not a good thing for a man his age to still be living with his mother. He had his own house so he wasn't lying when he said, "No, I have my own house, but she lives alone so I have to stop by often to check on her."

"That is wonderful. I took care of my mother until she died last year. She had a stroke and just slipped away one night." Robert felt good that he had gotten the worst of his life out in the open. He knew that he must find a way to ask for her number and ask her if she was free to date. He would have to hurry up before she bought her groceries and even worse, left the store. John thought, 'here I go.'

"Grace, I need to ask you something. Are you married or involved with someone?"

"No, I am not married or involved with anyone. Why do you ask?"

"I have been thinking about you a lot after I saw you here yesterday and was wondering if you would be willing to go to dinner with me."

"Before I answer, are you married or seeing anyone else?"

"No, I am not married or seeing anyone else. Me asking you to dinner doesn't prove that I am not married or seeing anyone else?"

"Not in today's society it does not. I know men who just like to date multiple people and/or are already married and still see other people. I just don't agree with that lifestyle."

"Neither do I Grace, neither do I. I am not that kind of man. So will you go out with me?"

"Yes, I would like to go out with you."

"How about next Friday or Saturday night?""

"Friday night would be great. Where shall I meet you?"

"I can pick you up."

"No, I prefer to have my own vehicle and meet you at a restaurant."

"I totally understand. Let's meet at Old Country Inn on the highway. Can I have your number just in case something happens and I can't make it or just want to talk? I will be happy to give you my cell number as well."

"Sure," They exchanged phone numbers and said their goodbyes. Grace was headed to the cashier to pay. John watched her all of the way to the check out. Grace's long brown hair, brown eyes, that red hooded coat and that bright smile will be haunting him until next Friday night. He really liked that she was secure in herself and had a standard with her life. Grace was her name. Finally. John lost his sense of direction and headed down the wrong aisle for the cinnamon rolls. Fortunately, no one saw him and he smiled in spite of himself and soon found his way. He was prouder than a peacock to have asked this young woman out and she said yes. She was a grandmother? The grandmothers today were getting younger and prettier. Grace's talkative grandson had been a God send that day. 'Thank you, Bradley,' John thought.

When John pulled in the driveway, there were no lights on in the house. John assumed that his mom was still asleep so he didn't go in the house right away. John parked his truck and walked to the flower bed to pull the remaining weeks to make it look neater. Winter was fast approaching. There would be snow on the ground soon and weeding would be over. He hadn't done anything inside or outside yesterday so he wanted to get something done today. John walked outside and Mr. Jones was headed to get his newspaper. Mr. Jones waved to John as usual. John waved back. This was the small-town way. When Mr. Jones got his paper, he walked toward John.

"How's it going John?"

"Fine, Mr. Jones, how's it going with you?"

"Fine. How's your mother doing today?"

"Well, she's doing better today. She had a fall when I came home yesterday morning from the grocery and I stayed home from work to take care of her."

"Sorry to hear about that John. You are a great son. Even without a wife and kids, you are committed to your mother and that's great. Have you ever thought about a family of your own?"

"Yes, lots of times. I even told my mom yesterday that I was going to start dating again and go on with my life, but she had that fall yesterday and I am re-thinking that idea."

"Why?"

"Because my mom needs me. My dad's been gone for more than twenty years, and she would be all alone without me."

"You know I have lived next door to your mom for many years and watched her keep you with her for more than twenty years now. Don't you think it's awful coincidental that she has a fall the day you tell her that you are going to start dating? I am not trying to start anything, but don't you think that's a little convenient?"

"Yes, it's interesting, but I really don't think my mom would do that."

"Okay just be careful. Mothers are tricky."

"Thanks for telling me, but not my mom. She really loves me."

Inside the house the phone rang and Helen Black answered after three rings because she was still groggy from sleep, "Hello."

"Helen, Bob just went to get the paper. How did everything go?" Helen woke up quickly at the sound of Mildred's voice.

"Girl, the plan worked beautifully. I bet he won't be going out with no woman anytime soon. I will have my son all to myself. He even stayed home from work yesterday to take care of me. He waited on me hand and foot."

"I am glad everything worked out for you but be careful because if this backfires, you could lose all the way around."

"I am not going to lose. I will win. John will be taking care of me until I die. He went to talking all about this life that he wanted for himself. Telling me that he was going to start dating and I was not going to call him so many times a day. I am going to start living back in my own house. Girl please. John is going to be right here with me, forever. Never to leave me."

"Okay, I am just saying. Be careful."

"Mildred, who are you telling to be careful?" Mildred nearly jumped out of her skin at the sound of Bob's voice.

"Nobody."

"Don't let me touch star 69, Mildred. What are you meddling in that is none of your business?"

"Nothing."

"Mildrrreed?"

"Okay. It was Helen. She is convinced that John is going to start dating and leave her. She has tricked him into believing that she fell on yesterday when he went to the store. I told her to be careful."

"I thought something was fishy when he said that she fell and now he was not going to be dating anyone and just stay at the house to take care of her. That is horrible for Helen to do that to him."

"I know. I tried to warn her."

"Warn her or encourage her?"

"Bob, I really tried to warn her."

"Well, I must confess that I tried to warn him about her as well. He is convinced that she loves him and would never try to do anything like that. In his words, 'I really don't think my mom would do that.' Mildred, as much as we hate it, we are going to have to let nature take its course. Agreed."

"But what happens when…"

"What happens when nothing. Agreed."

"Okay. Bob, I agree, but I really was trying to help John."

"Let's eat breakfast and stop talking about the neighbors."

John went back in the house to an awakened mother. "Mom, how are you feeling today?"

"I'm alright," she said weakly and moving very slowly. "With a great son like you, I am better than alright."

"Mom, I want to ask you something. If I met somebody, would you mind if I dated them?"

"No, I don't mind if you date, but I would want to meet her first." Helen thought, 'Where did this come from about dating someone. She thought she had swashed the notion of dating with the fall on yesterday. She had hoped that would be enough. Apparently not. She would have to come up with another plan.'

"No problem, Mom. I wouldn't be serious about anybody unless you met them first."

'Great,' John thought. 'I will pretend to work late on Friday night and hopefully bring Grace to meet mom on the next date after.' He sat watching television with his mom, but the television was watching him. The rest of the night, John thought about Grace constantly and counted the hours until he would see her on Friday. His mother felt like she could walk in any door at any time so he closed his door and locked it. He wanted to relieve his own aroused erection himself in the privacy without his mom interrupting as she had done countless times before. His dream was to be able to have an actual woman fulfill those needs without having to use his own hand. Oh my, he couldn't wait for the day. He just laid back on his pillows, closed his eyes and let the hand do the job for now.

Meanwhile, James picked up Candy at the corner of Main and 2nd Street two hours earlier right outside the Pleasantview Apartments. She was wearing no leggings, a short sweater top, boots and a knee length black coat. When she got in the car, she leaned over and gave James a hot wet kiss which was only a prelude of the night to come. He put one hand in her hair and the other up her sweater and there was nothing there but skin. He got aroused at the mere thought of having sex with Candy. He turned the corner in the alley, unzipped his pants and she rode him to explosion with her butt hitting the steering wheel. There was no time to lean the seat back make room so the first time that night was uncomfortable for her, but heaven for him. Once they got to the house, his nerves were on calm and he was ready for dinner. He picked up two complete steak dinners from the local Texas Roadhouse and was reheating them in the oven on low to give the house the fresh cooked smell. He already had plans to go to a Waffle House in Louisville for breakfast before taking Candy back to her apartment. James had it so bad that he already had lined up a girl named

Jasmine to be with on Saturday afternoon and Saturday night. He planned on being on sex overload by the time Linda got home on Sunday afternoon from her weekend with his son at college.

"Wow, Jimmy, this is a lovely home you have." James had come home early and removed any pictures of the family from the walls and the shelves. He didn't want Candy to know anything about him except the bedroom and satisfying his little jimmy in his pants. That's all she needed to concern herself with tonight and tomorrow. He had the house to himself and it was going to be sweet.

"Thanks baby. I've lived here for about 20 years now." Candy never asked any man she was with about their family unless they wanted to talk about it. She wasn't a prostitute on the corner, but she knew how to please a man. At one time, Candy wanted to get married but there seemed to be no takers. Her insatiable appetite for sex didn't make her the marrying kind. She always thought being a freak in the bed would be attractive, but it just didn't work out for her.

"Wow! What smells so good?" Candy asked.

"It's a complete steak dinner with salad. I got an ice cream pie for dessert among other things."

"That's sounds great."

"You hungry?"

"Yes."

"I guess you are hungry since we have already worked up an appetite." James took Candy's hand and pulled her to him for another hot kiss. Hands started going all over each other's bodies. "I don't want to start and then stop to eat so let's eat first."

"Okay. If that's what you want, but you know, big daddy, I can go anytime you want."

"Don't tempt me."

With that said, Candy removed her sweater and crooked her finger toward James. It only took James a few seconds to cross the room and with her boots still on, took her right there on the floor of the living room. The next time they were on the couch and the last time was back on the floor. Both wrapped in the Afghan crocheted by Linda's mom, James led Candy to the kitchen. He was like a fish out of water in the kitchen, but he managed to prepare their plates without too much mess and served them both. James was truly out of character being so willing to serve someone he barely knew when he barely spoke to the person he was married to. James had the ultimate disrespect for Linda and his house. He left the dishes, food and all of the trash out in the kitchen.

His main focus was having sex with Candy. He did just that all over the house from the floor and on just about every piece of furniture that would hold them both. The staircase was not off limits or any of the appliances in the house. They were both insatiable. About 4:00 a.m., they ended their sexual escapades in the shower for one last round before collapsing in the bed that he shared with Linda.

The next day, James had forgotten all about going to Waffle House or the afternoon delight and tryst with Jasmine at 2:00 p.m. He turned over and pulled Candy closer. The curtains were drawn so they didn't realize that it was already noon. The weather service had predicted snow to begin around 1:00 p.m. that afternoon, but these two were oblivious to the weather report.

"Dad?" James felt the bed shake and woke up with a start to see both of his sons standing over him, watching him cuddle naked in the bed with Candy and not their mother.

"Will and Stephen, what are you two doing here?"

In unison, they said, "What are you doing?" Two half grown young men were confused, angry, disappointed and hurt by their father and also wondering what he was doing in the bed with another woman in their family home.

"I can explain."

"You are going to explain what you are doing naked in a bed with another woman that you share with our mother!" William exclaimed.

"Lower your voice son!" James demanded.

"You're married with children?" Candy asked.

"Yes, I am married, and these are my two sons," James stated.

"Explain to us why you would cheat on our mother who has given her life for you and us," Stephen added.

"Listen, I am still your father," James insisted.

"Barely. What father would do this in his own home? You don't cheat in your own house with a whore in your wife's bed," William insisted.

"Excuse me, I am not a whore," Candy interjected, "I am a person too."

"Just shut up Candy! This doesn't concern you."

"Shut up! You didn't say shut up or stop or don't when we were screwing all over this house last night."

"Shut up these are my children."

"They don't look like children to me. These are grown ass men who need to know exactly what kind of father you really are. We have been meeting like this in hotels all over town."

"Shut up! Bitch!"

"Bitch! You calling me a bitch? What the hell? I am out. Give me this blanket so I can go downstairs, get my clothes and go home. Give me money to get a cab," Candy pulled the blanket off of the bed which left James naked because the sheet had fallen on the floor. James jumped up to grab a pair of underwear out of his second drawer. He yelled out as Candy grabbed her purse and went down the stairs to find her sweater, boots and coat.

"Bitch, I ain't giving you nothing. You got a steak dinner last night, as much dick as you can handle and that should half way satisfy you."

William and Stephen stood by and watched this exchange in shock. They were amazed by their father's conversation with this woman.

"Why are you home Stephen? I thought you were going away for the entire weekend?" James asked trying to change the subject.

"Dad, you haven't listened to the weather because you have been so busy, but there is a blizzard about to start at 1:00 p.m. The First Baptist Church of Roberts Junction got the weather report and cut the trip short to get us home by noon."

"Listen young man, don't smart off to me. I am still your father," James insisted.

Stephen rolled his eyes and turned to look out the window saying nothing more.

"Why are you home, William?" James inquired.

"We lost the game, and it is Becky's birthday. So, I came home for the party last night, to take her to the movies and then go back to school some time tonight. I came home to get more clean clothes. That doesn't explain what this is about," William wasn't fooled about his father's tactics to change the subject and not give a full explanation.

"It's about nothing son. She was just a fling. It means nothing."

"She said that you met and had sex often in hotels. Is that true?" Stephen inquired.

"Is she the only one or are there others?" William inquired.

James may not have passed the entrance exam to law school, but his sons knew how to attack him with questioning.

James avoided their questions by spouting a bunch of, 'well' or 'sort of' or 'it doesn't mean anything' or 'it wasn't really like that' answers to his sons. James had been caught red handed by his own sons and could not talk his way out of it. He was stammering and stuttering, but he was not sorry or repentant. He knew that he had lost his sons' respect. He didn't know how he would ever regain it.

To the boys, their mother was everything to them even if she meant nothing to their dad. What was to come of their family? Would they join the statistic of other children with divorced parents? Their dad wasn't even trying to cover it and tell them not to tell their mother. Did he care so little for their mom and them?

Downstairs, Candy found James' wallet and took all of his money while his sons interrogated him upstairs. She didn't care if she ever saw him again. She opened the front door, walked out, called a friend and waited in the snow.

"Dad, have you even thought about Mom out in this weather?" William asked.

"She could be caught in this blizzard, and she doesn't even have a cell phone!" Stephen added.

"No, sons, I haven't thought about your mother at all this weekend. It was all about me. She's a grown woman and can take care of herself. Stephen, I haven't bought your mom a cell phone because she didn't really need a cell phone. Now that I think about it, she can buy her own damn cell phone with her own little money."

"For real, dad. This is the 21st century and everybody has a cell phone. William and I have cell phones, why doesn't Mom?" Stephen asked.

"This is pointless," William said and the boys left their dad and went into their joint bedroom.

"This is ridiculous William. Dad doesn't care about our mother. How did that happen? When did they fall out of love? Did you see it happen?" Stephen asked.

"Neither of us saw it because our mother is that great and held the house together while our dad was doing who knows what with who knows who."

"You think that it's been going on for months?"

"Maybe even years."

"What do we do?"

"Nothing but watch Mom closer."

"What if she decides to leave him?"

"Let her. We can't be selfish. He is selfish enough for all of us. It is not fair for Mom to be in a relationship with somebody who doesn't care about her. We should love her enough to let her make the decision and stand by the decision she makes."

"I don't want to have a broken family," Stephen said.

"Stephen, it's broken already," William replied.

Chapter 9 – Pride Fallen

Across town, Jamie woke to the beautiful sight of snow beginning to fall outside her apartment window. She loved snow. She had always loved snow as a child. It always looked like God was covering the earth with a white blanket. She pulled her blanket and comforter over her body and turned on the television to watch the news. What had happened in the world today?

Her phone suddenly rang.

"Hello."

"Is this Jamie Miller?"

"My name is David Noles, and I am calling on behalf of your parents, Frank and Martha Miller."

"Yes, has something happened to my parents?"

"Yes, I am sorry to report that they were killed in a car accident by a drunk driver last night."

"Oh, no!" Jamie screamed so loud that she thought her vocal cords would rip out of her throat. She wanted to rip her heart out of her chest to somehow make the pain go away but, it wouldn't. This young man's words felt like a knife literally cutting her heart out of her chest.

"Their bodies are at the morgue now, and the G. H. Herrmann Funeral is in charge of carrying out their pre-arranged funeral arrangements. They need you to call them sometime today to make an appointment. I am so sorry to have to call you, because I had all intentions of coming to Roberts Junction to see you in person. The Department of Transportation has closed the roads here in Indianapolis and advising no one to travel until tomorrow. If you would like, I could try to come to Roberts Junction tomorrow or Monday to escort you back to Indianapolis or can you get here on your own?"

"I can get there, I think."

"Can you get a pen and paper and write this number down?"

"I can try, but right now I think I am going to lose my mind first and then call."

"I would be losing my mind, too. I will hold on while you find a pen." Jamie turned her usually neat room upside down trying to find a pen. She went throughout her house and David could hear her in the background say, "Mommy and Daddy gone." She searched throughout her small apartment only to find a pen in her kitchen.

"I am back."

"First, here is the number to the funeral home and the contact is Ms. Martha Hermann, 317-555-1233. Secondly, this is my cell number, 317-500-7898. If you have any questions, day or night, call me. My name again is David."

"Okay, I will, bye," When Jamie hung up the phone she screamed again. She screamed because she never went back home to say sorry. She screamed because she never told them that she really loved them and had no real reason why she did all of those horrible things in her past. She screamed because now she was really alone. She sat in her bed all day, screaming and crying. She screamed so loud that her neighbor knocked on her door to make sure that she was alright.

"Jamie are you alright?" Mrs. Mason called out through her front door. Mrs. Mason lived in the apartment underneath Jamie and could hear everything that went on in her apartment through the vents above.

"No, I am not alright, Mrs. Mason. I just got a call that my parents were killed in a car accident by a drunk driver!" Jamie yelled through the door. She hadn't gotten dressed or showered, or she would have opened the door to talk to Mrs. Mason.

"I am sorry baby; I'll be praying for you when I get to church tomorrow morning."

"Thank you and ignore my screams and crying."

"That's alright baby, Get it all out. Get it all out."

At 4:30 p.m., Jamie called the funeral home. This was the hardest thing she would ever do. Why didn't she reach out to them sooner? There was nothing stopping her from reaching out except her pride. What good was pride now that her parents were gone?

In Bloomington, Linda woke up slowly. She was acclimating herself to her surroundings. The smell of breakfast filled the air and brought Linda out of Robert's large bed and into the kitchen. She put on the jersey that he dressed her in last night. She didn't bring house shoes. Fortunately, most of the house was carpeted except for the kitchen, so Linda would be fine barefoot. Linda was the cook in her house. She always cooked. She spoiled her sons and James so that they never lifted a finger to help do anything in the house except consume. When Linda walked in the kitchen, Robert turned and smiled at the sight of her. She walked down the counter going from plate to plate to see the bacon, biscuits, eggs, French toast, pancakes, hash browns and fresh brewed coffee.

"Good morning," Robert bent down and kissed her thoroughly and then returned to checking his griddle.

"Oh, my goodness, Robert, what have you done?"

"I have made a breakfast meal fit for a queen. You are truly a phenomenal woman. Have a seat."

"This is not a meal but a feast. What I can do to help? I am not used to all of this service."

"That's the reason why you deserve to get this type of service," Where Robert found a rose, Linda did not know. There was a long stem red rose in a small red glass vase sitting on the table. "Do you like French toast or pancakes? Scrambled or over easy eggs? It's your choice."

"Whatever and however you fix it, I am eating it. I am really not a picky eater. Food is food to me. Where did you get the rose?"

"A little birdie brought it to me and said that somebody special in my house was a rose and should receive one. I heard the weather report and realized that I was going to need food in the house and went to the store before the rush," Robert answered with a smile. He couldn't sleep. He wanted to make the time when Linda woke up even more special than their night together. He realized there were no groceries in the refrigerator. The trip had been unplanned so the service had not been called. He was so excited that he smiled all the way to the store. As he walked every aisle, he tried to imagine what foods she would eat and really enjoy. Linda had said that 'she wasn't a picky eater,' but he didn't care what she said, he would take great care in selecting what he served her.

"Thank you," Linda smiled as she put the rose to her nose and smelled its unique fragrance.

"Here we go," Robert had a beautiful table set with place settings in rust and brown colors with the full linens to match. The Christmas decorations and linens were already in the store so he was able to buy the fall-colored linens on sale. Thank goodness because he just had to buy everything and set the table just like the display in the store. He strategically placed all of the food on the table in arms reach of Linda.

"Wow, this looks incredible. So much food I think it will feed an army."

Robert took her hand in his and said a quick prayer over the food, "Thank you God for Linda and bless this food. Amen."

"Amen. I don't think God would approve of what we were doing last night."

"Probably not but I still thank Him for you and the food we are about to eat. We will worry about confessing and receiving forgiveness later for what we did last night. I don't regret anything."

"Me either," Linda didn't want to say it, but she really didn't know how she was going to move forward after last night. What would the boys think? How and where would she live? What did her relationship with Robert really mean? Had she been a one-night stand? Why was she even thinking of that right now?

Robert broke through her thoughts saying, "Well, right now we are going to eat this wonderful breakfast and enjoy watching the SNOW!" Robert got up and drew back the curtains in the breakfast nook. There was at least 6 inches on the ground.

"Snow! When did the snow start?"

"About an hour ago."

"I love snow but how much and how long? I need to be home and go to work on Monday."

"Don't worry you can stay as long as you need to. You are not going anywhere for a while because the highway is closed. So, eat up and enjoy the snow as it comes down and piles up."

Linda didn't know whether to be happy for the snow or happy she couldn't go home right away. As for right now, she was going to stay put and just be happy. Robert and Linda finished breakfast, cleaned up the kitchen and retrieved her belongings out of her car. She showered and they tidied up the house together. Robert pulled out his pictures from college and other accomplishments and shared them with Linda. As the hours progressed, they learned more and more about each other. It was amazing how comfortable they were together. Each told stories of the past 20 plus years involving their lives, children, hopes and dreams. The snow had picked up and was estimated to snow at least a foot before stopping this evening. Everything was closed in Bloomington and the news asked that only emergency vehicles be on the roads. They were laying on the couch looking into the blazing fire in each other's arms. They were wrapped in blankets like a cocoon facing each other. Soft touches and kisses were exchanged while gazing into each other's eyes. This sweet loving made Linda want Robert even more.

"I have one question for you, Mr. Matthews."

"Okay, ask."

"Why haven't you married anyone, or why aren't you currently in a serious relationship?"

"The truth?"

"Yes, I want the truth."

"I don't want to be with anybody else. I have always loved you and only wanted to marry you."

"You are lying."

"No, I am not lying."

"Then what was the one-night stand about with Brooks?"

"A challenge."

"Challenge?"

"Yes, she challenged me. I didn't see the trap. She said that I was probably gay if I didn't sleep with her. I was weak and fell for it. It was the biggest mistake of my life. In the end, I lost you. I had plans to marry you after college. I knew that I wanted to be a lawyer but after being with Brooks and the birth of Jennifer, I just couldn't put you through that. You were dating James and I knew that I didn't have a chance after that. I should have told Brooks, 'no I am not gay' and let the chips fall where they may. I was young and stupid. She later told me that she was jealous of the two of us and wanted to find some way to break us up."

"She succeeded. I think James came after me because he wanted to take something away from you. I think that we were both tricked."

"I have a wonderful daughter and from what you tell me, you have two fantastic sons."

"I do. Speaking of sons, I think I should check on them both. William went back last night and I wanted to tell him to just stay in Roberts Junction and not come back to school until the weather cleared."

"Use my phone." Just then Robert's cell phone rang. He left the room so Linda could have her privacy.

Linda picked up Robert's phone and dialed William's number first.

"Hello."

"William, this is Mom."

"Mom, are you okay?"

"I am fine. I just borrowed someone's phone."

"Who?"

"Nobody that you know. I don't have a phone so I have to do what I have to do."

"Right, we need to get you a phone right away. When are you coming home?"

"I don't need a phone right away, but I do need one soon. I don't know right now because the roads are closed. It's about a foot of snow on the ground here. There goes my little shopping trip. I guess I should have come home with you last night."

"Well, it's probably best that you are there and didn't come home today. Do you have enough money, food and gas?" William thought quickly of the sight of seeing his father in bed with another woman. Thank goodness mom didn't come home.

"Look at my grown-up son caring about his mother. Yes, sweetie, I am fine."

"I love you, Mom," William wanted to cry. He was so upset with his father and hurt for his mother, but it couldn't be helped. Whatever he needed to do to support his mother he would. His father had been his hero. Now he was just a man that he didn't like any more.

"I love you too baby. Is it a lot of snow there?"

"It's not as much snow here just about 6 inches, but they have closed the roads on this end as well going north. I hope that they will have the roads open so I can go back to school on Monday. Stephen and I are hanging out at Ryan's until you get back. Ryan's parents are not going to let Ryan drive until the roads are clear anyway. Ryan is a good driver, but it is better to be safe than sorry."

"Is that okay with Ryan's parents for both of you to stay there? What did your dad say?"

"Ryan's parents said that we could stay as long as we like. Dad didn't say nothing. He is fine home alone. We didn't ask him. We just left because he was sleep or in the shower. I don't remember." After William and Stephen realized that there was no getting any straight answers from their father, William and Stephen went and packed clean clothes in a bag and left. Neither son said so much as a word to James prior to leaving the house.

"Tell Ryan's parents for me that I greatly appreciate them allowing you guys to stay."

"I will."

"Well, I don't want to tie up this person's phone so I will hang up now. Tell Stephen that I love him too and I will see you guys on Monday or very soon."

Linda hung up the phone and sat on the couch just looking into the fire. She didn't know where Robert was taking his call, but she would give him his privacy.

Robert was in his office adjacent to the master bedroom on the phone, "David, did she call the funeral home yet?"

"Yes, I called them back. The funeral director said that she had called and let them know that she would be coming to Indianapolis as soon as the roads opened. I am going to call her back in a few minutes to check on her and see if she has any questions."

"It might be good if you just drove her back to Roberts Junction and then stayed a couple of days to check on the office in Roberts Junction. I have planned for you to be in charge of that office and you need to look around and see where you want to live."

"I appreciate the opportunity to head the Roberts Junction office, Mr. Matthews, and I won't let you down. I will offer to drive Ms. Miller back to Roberts Junction, but she may refuse." David said.

"If she refuses, follow her back in your car, but I need you on site next week. We need to move forward and not miss a beat with our clients there and the possibility of a new client."

"Yes sir, I am on it. A new client?" David asked.

"I will let you know about the new client when I know more. I'm just thinking ahead right now."

"Sure. I'll wait for the details later," David had come a long way from the trailer parks of Indianapolis' east side. He had lifted himself up from his past. Where he was raised was not going to define him. He was given an opportunity for a scholarship to college at IUPUI to get out of his situation after high school and he took it. He was single, no children and not tied to anyone. This was another opportunity to move forward, so he was going to take this challenge by the horns and prove that a boy from the wrong side of the tracks could make good and rise to be a managing partner in a very prestigious law firm.

"Be safe, David, and keep me posted when you are leaving Indianapolis."

"Yes, sir, I will. You be safe as well." Robert Matthews had not only been a law mentor to David, but secretly he felt like Mr. Matthews was his father. He wanted to make him proud of him. His own father died at the hand of a drunk driver. His mother died a few years later of breast cancer because she refused to go get herself checked out. Both died needlessly and over something that could have been helped. David realized that he would not live or die like that.

Robert pressed 'end' on his cell phone and came out of his office to find Linda. Linda. If someone had told him six months ago that he would have made love to Linda Harris all night long in his house and his bed, he would have called them a liar. He was in heaven. Robert had to figure a way to get her in his life forever he thought to himself as he walked back down the hall to the living room. Every moment in her presence was precious. He was anxious to get back to her.

"Linda?" Robert said her name somewhere between a whisper, question and a longing.

"Yes, I am here." Linda turned at his voice.

"Yes, you are. Are you okay?" Robert asked as he stood in the door way just looking at her sitting on his couch. She was looking at him, but still seemed so far away. He hoped nothing happened to her sons while she was here. He never wanted her to feel guilty being with him. Linda turned back to look into the fire.

"I'm fine, but concerned. The boys are safe. They are staying at William's best friend's house. Ryan Prather."

"That's good that they are safe. I didn't know Ryan Prather was from Roberts Junction. He always said he was from Southern Indiana, but I never nailed down the exact city or town. He is one of the young men that I am mentoring," Robert had crossed the room and sat down on the arm of the couch opposite Linda.

"It's a small world. You know sometimes young people don't always want to recognize the small town that they are from."

"You are right. What else did your son say?" Robert inquired trying to keep Linda talking so she wouldn't be so worried.

"It is still snowing there and about six inches on the ground. The roads are closed there, but it concerns me that they aren't staying at our house. I just think that is interesting."

"Oh, you know how young people are. They probably just wanted to hang out since you were out of town."

"Yes, you're probably right, but he said that he hadn't talked to his father to ask permission or even notify him that they were staying over there."

"They are growing up."

"Yes, but they are not full grown yet and have to tell somebody about their whereabouts."

"They told their mother," Robert moved closer to Linda on the couch just in case she needed him.

"You are right. Everything okay with you?"

"Yes. David Noles was on the phone. He is one of the firm's Senior Associates. He is working on something for a client of ours. As a matter of fact, my plan is for him to head the office in Roberts Junction. Maybe you can give him some pointers on where to live and/or introduce him to people. He is single, no children, an only child and a nice guy."

"I will have to keep him away from Jamie Miller at the Goodwill," Linda smiled thinking about Jamie and her antics.

"Jamie Miller works at the Goodwill?"

"That was the young woman who was all up in my business and looking you up and down when you were in the store. She came from the back room and almost ran over you with the rack of shirts."

"Right. Roberts Junction is too small. Well, I am not really supposed to say anything, but since you know her, her parents were killed in a car accident last night. David was giving me an update on contacting Jamie Miller because her parents were our clients. We are taking care of their estate." Linda rushed into Robert's arms at that knowledge of the death of Jamie's parents. Robert cradled Linda like a baby. He cupped her head against his shoulder and gently rubbed her back for comfort. How he was going to let this beautiful, sensitive woman walk out his front door taking his heart with her, he did not know.

"No, that is terrible. I don't know why I am so emotional, but I feel so sorry for Jamie. She didn't talk about her parents. She is alone, single and has no children. She told me that she is an only child. She rarely spoke of her parents because they were somehow estranged. How did they die?" Linda asked.

"Drunk driver," Robert said in a somber tone still cradling Linda.

Linda said, "No!" so loud that it resonated throughout the living room. She was visibly moved by the news. "She is all alone now except for us at the store. I miss my dad every day and I know how that feels. You think I should call her?"

"Yes, you should, but give her a few minutes because David is calling to check on her right now. She has made funeral arrangements over the phone and can't get to Indianapolis because of the roads. Also, you have to call her and be natural. You cannot let on that you know about her parents. Let her tell you the news about her parents. I have breached confidentiality enough just by telling you this much."

"You are right, I will let her tell me. Thank you for your trust in me."

"Thank you too for trusting me. This trust journey requires that we trust in each other. Look at me," Linda turned to face Robert as he spoke, "No matter what happens next, we are on this journey together and you are not alone."

"I really don't want to think about what's next, but I am thankful that you are there for me and I'm not alone."

"Sometimes I hate being alone with no parents or siblings. That is the reason why I work so hard and fill my days with so many activities. My house is a refuge of sorts, but mostly a hotel to change clothes and sleep."

"You could have someone that you come home to every night, like me, and still feel alone. Believe you me, that life is just as miserable," Linda and Robert wrapped themselves again in the Afghan on the couch and watched the fire for a while. Robert realized that after this time with Linda, he never wanted to be alone again. Linda realized that she had been alone in a marriage for more than 20 years. After this weekend, she never wanted to be alone with someone again. Each in their own thoughts of what to do next, held each other tighter and closer while watching the fire burn bright.

Chapter 10 – Mother Black

John was going stir crazy in the house. It had stopped snowing for a few minutes so he decided to start shoveling snow at only ten-minute intervals. He had read about so many men having heart attacks while shoveling snow that he knew that he would go slow and have all day to get it done. His mom was resting. Breakfast and lunch had been eaten, dishes were washed and put away.

John had only been shoveling a short time when he heard a dog barking in the direction of the street in front of his mom's house. This wasn't unusual in Roberts Junction. He looked up and saw the dog dart out in front of a car. The car missed the dog, but the car began to slide sideways and head to the ditch. The front two wheels were off of the road into the ditch because of the ice at the stop sign. John grabbed the handle of his shovel and headed toward the car to help. Mr. Jones was watching too from his front door and came out on the porch. Even though Mr. Jones was closer to the car from his house, he was much older and would be of limited physical help to John.

"John be careful," Mr. Jones called out.

"Okay, Mr. Jones." John walked over to the car door and knocked on the window. "Are you alright?" It was a woman driving in the car alone. When she looked toward the window, John said, "Grace?"

"John? Thank God it is you."

"Yes, it is me. Can you get the door opened?" John couldn't believe that Grace was right here in his front yard. What is the likelihood that it would happen? She had been haunting his dream last night, but now she was physically in his presence. He didn't know her that well yet, but he was glad that God picked this street for her to need his help.

"No, it appears stuck," Fortunately, the car slid off of the road in slow motion. If the car had suffered any harder impact, the air bags could have opened and injured Grace. John was thankful for that.

"Press the button to unlock the door," John and Grace both heard the popping sound of the unlocking of the car door. "The door sounds unlocked. I am going to try to pull the door open and you try to push it open toward me. We are going to do it together on 3. Here we go, 1, 2, and 3," John pulled as hard as he could while Grace made all efforts to push, but the driver's door nor the passenger door would open. Her car was a two door, otherwise he would have tried one of the backseat doors.

"Mr. Jones, call the fire department. Her doors won't open to get her out," John called out.

"Hold on Grace. The neighbor is going to call the fire department to come and possibly cut you out of the car."

"Oh, no! My car will be ruined!" Grace exclaimed.

"Just calm down. It will be alright. The most important thing is that you are safe and not to worry about the car right now. Remember, we haven't been on our date yet. I am not going to let anything happen to you before then," Grace smiled oh so slightly, "That's better. I made you smile and that's all that matters." It took only minutes after Mr. Jones made the call for the emergency crews to come down the street. The fire department was not that far away when they heard the sirens coming down the street. The fireman said that it appeared that the door was jammed from the force, but was not frozen because they were unlocked.

John's mom, Helen, looked out the window at her son, helping a young woman out of her car. She did not like the way the young woman hugged John or the way John was hugging her back. Who was she, and why was she hugging her son? Maybe she was just thankful for his help. John was such a good boy to her, but she wanted him all to herself and no one else.

"Thank you, John, for helping me," Grace turned to the firemen and thanked them as well. The tow truck was coming up the street to tow her car away to the local repair shop of her choice, "Well, I guess I will ride with the tow truck and see about my car."

"Let me take you and then bring you home. Why don't you come in and meet my mom?"

"I look a mess. Maybe some other time."

"No, I think right now is simply a perfect time," John stayed with Grace while she explained to the tow truck driver where she wanted the car towed to and walked with John back to his mom's house. Helen was standing in the doorway when they came onto the porch.

"Mom? I have somebody that I want you to meet."

"Oh, yeah?"

"This is Grace. This is the young woman who just had the accident in the car. I am going to take her to the gas station where they are towing her car and then home."

"Hello," Grace said with a smile.

"Hello. Gretchen did you say?"

"No, ma'am it's Grace."

"Oh, I am sorry Grace. John, you are going out in this snow? Doesn't she have a husband, honey, who can come and pick her up?"

"No, she doesn't have a husband. I am going to take her to her car and then home. I will be fine in the snow."

"You know they are predicting more snow and the highways are closed."

"Yes, Mom but with my truck. I will be fine," John was too happy about this young woman for Helen to rest at ease. She had to get a message to this young woman about any future intentions with her son and by the looks of things, she was almost too late.

"Uh, John, can you do me one favor and go out and get the paper for me before you go?"

"Yes, ma'am," John walked toward the mailbox while he left Grace alone with his mother.

"Excuse me young lady. Do you have any children?"

"Yes, ma'am, I have a daughter."

"Oh, so you will understand what I am about to say. Let's get one thing straight. I don't know if you have known him before this little accident of yours, but he seems just too happy to be giving you a ride in this blizzard to take care of your business. But, let me tell you that if you have any intentions of dating my son, get them out of your mind, now. My son lives with me, and will live with me until I die. I have all intentions of keeping my son as close to me as possible. He is all I have."

"I thought he had his own place."

"Oh, so you do know my son before now."

"Yes, ma'am, we met in the grocery store this week."

"Well, he does have his own house, but it is basically closed up because I wanted him to live with me. What I want goes, you hear? I will win and you will not. I don't care what you try to do. Understand?"

"Yes, ma'am, I understand. Since I probably won't see you again, let me tell you something. I don't know what will happen in the future of our relationship, but you could have a son, daughter and grandchildren if you let him go. Think about that. Not allowing him to live happily, is cruel and not what I would call a good mother."

"Well, look at you talking smart to me when you don't even know me."

"Yes, but I have seen your kind before. It is mothers like you that is the reason for my divorce. Goodbye. I am going to wait by John's truck," Just then John opened the back door with the paper in his hand. Grace was about to slide past John when his voice caused her to stop.

"Grace, I need for you to stand in here for a minute."

"I think that it's best for me to go outside," Grace stated.

"No, I need for you to stand here and listen to what I have to say," Grace turned at the tone in John's voice. She closed the screen door and stood just inside the doorway. "Mother, I heard what you said to Grace. I almost went all of the way to the box but remembered that Mary Jane's son puts the papers on the porch during a blizzard. I heard every word through the back screen door. You forgot to close it, you were so busy telling Grace a thing or two. I don't know Grace well yet, but through this accident, I am about to get to know her very well if she will let me. Mr. Jones tried to warn me, but I told him not my mother, she would never do anything like that. You don't even know Grace, but you believe that someone is trying to take me away from you. I will always be your son, but I have a life to live. Now, that I think about it, you didn't really fall yesterday, it was fake. Tell me the truth."

"John, do you really think I would do something like that?" Helen batted her eyes rapidly at him with a voice that was meant to sound weak.

"Mother, for once tell me the truth. Don't try to manipulate me."

"You just had to stay! I can't let you go too! Your father left me and you are all I have left!" Helen shouted.

"Yes, now that is gone too. Goodbye Mother. You have food and everything you need in the refrigerator. The Jones' are nearby if you have a REAL emergency and if something else comes up, call 911. I need a break. I need some time away from you. I will always love you, but right now, I don't like you. I will be back for my things sometime later or tomorrow or maybe some other time next week. I haven't decided yet. Let's go Grace."

"NO!!! John No! John No! Don't go, please don't go!" John could still hear his mother screaming and beating on the window as he cleared the snow off of his truck and let Grace in on the passenger side. He couldn't give in. He had to fight for his life. He didn't really know if Grace was the one, but she was the one who let him see his mother for who she really is. Grace was the one sitting by his side in this truck right now and that's all he knew. He would give his mother a week or two to get used to the idea before he came back, but today was the day. He would always love his mother, but he had to walk away now or it may never happen. He remembered that he left his phone on the table. He would cancel that number, get another company and start all over. Once in a life time chance for a new life, new woman, new phone and a new day.

When they arrived at the auto repair shop, it was open. There were so many cars on his lot that had been towed there that day that the owner didn't know when he would get to Grace's car. Grace was visibly upset and frustrated but knew that it couldn't be helped, "Oh man, if that dog just hadn't run out in front of my car. I was doing so good getting done what I needed done to get in the house before the storm."

"I need to find that dog, hug him and find the biggest bone to thank him," John said simply.

"You okay John?" Grace asked timidly.

"Yes and no."

"I can't tell you how sorry I am for all of this. I should one day apologize to your mom for the way I said what I said."

"Maybe, but right now I just have to get away. Do you have to go home right away?"

"No, what did you have in mind?"

"I need to go to my house and check on things. That is where I am going to be sleeping tonight. I need a new phone. I need to go to the grocery store, get some clothes for the next couple of days. Are you okay with hanging out with me? Kind of having our date a week early? This isn't really what I had in mind for you to see me like this, but who could have planned this?"

"Not in a million years. I would love to. I need for my daughter to have a minute to herself with her son. I need to get away from the constant questions of a three-year-old and be with a real grown up for a while," Grace giggled slightly and John smiled.

"Thank you."

Chapter 11 - David

"Hello." Jamie answered her phone still in shock from the news of her parents' death.

"Jamie? Hello this is David. I am calling to check on you."

"Thanks David, but I am okay. I called the funeral home and don't know when I am going to get there because of this snow. I am not really good at driving in snow."

"Do you think that you can get the bus to Indianapolis?"

"Yes, I guess so. How will I get home?"

"If you don't mind, I have to come back to Roberts Junction to take care of some business. Maybe we could ride together. With this snow, leave your car in Roberts Junction and I can take you back home after you have finished your business here."

"I think that would be fine. I don't think my nerves could take the snow drive and taking care of my parents' business too."

"You have my number in your phone. Call me and give me the details of when your bus should arrive."

"How will I know you?"

"I am a tall guy, but people tell me that there is something familiar about me when they meet me."

"Okay. I don't know how to thank you."

"You just did. I am doing my job and so sorry that I had to be the one to give you this kind of news. Maybe another time there will be something better to call you about."

"Maybe. Thanks again. We will talk soon, after I make arrangements."

"Be careful if you are going out today for any reason."

"You too." Jamie hung up the phone and realized that there was something familiar about his voice, but her mind wasn't clear enough to place it. There was so much for Jamie to do. She had a bus to catch and needed to get the price of a ticket. The phone rang again with a private number listed. Jamie didn't know anyone with a private number listing so she almost didn't answer it until her curiosity got the best of her.

"Hello."

"Hello Jamie?"

"Linda is this you? You never call me at home?"

"Just checking on you. I am still out of town and stuck in this snow. How are you?"

"This snow is something isn't it. I love snow but I don't know about this much."

"Right. How are you?"

"Not good, girl."

"What's up?" Linda tried to make her voice sound light, but inside she was holding her breath for what was coming next.

"My parents were killed last night by a drunk driver."

"No, Jamie. That is terrible. When and where?"

"According to the lawyer, they were riding down the highway and someone was driving drunk and came across the median and hit them in a head on collision. They were both killed instantly."

"Drunk driver. That is terrible. I know I can't do much because I am stuck in the snow, but I hope that I can do something when I get back in town," Robert was gently rubbing her back while she was talking on the phone, but stopped to go and poke the fire so it wouldn't go down. With the poke still in his hand, he sat on the floor listening to Linda's response and sometimes, no response at all. He loved her. He didn't know how to tell her, but he loved her just the same. She would have to go back to Roberts Junction, but how he would do that he didn't know. Somehow, he had to make her know how much he really loved her.

"Linda, right now I can't think of anything that you can do for me. I have food and everything. I just have to buy a bus ticket to Indianapolis and I have that too. Just pray for me and think good thoughts. I have no one, but me now," Jamie began to cry and so did Linda.

Linda was crying thinking about Jamie and herself. She was thinking about having to go back to Roberts Junction and face James. She didn't want to go back to James, she wanted to be with Robert. How would that happen? She didn't know if it was the right time to tell Robert or not, but somehow, she had to make him understand just how much she wanted to be with him.

Jamie continued, "It is amazing how death can change you. Being alone can really change you. I don't want to cry again but, I can't help it. It is too fresh. My biggest regret is that I have regret. I didn't connect with them when I should. I didn't tell them sorry when I should have. I tried to, but I really didn't make them understand me. I just came to Roberts Junction and hid. I got a job at the Goodwill to hide.

No one would come looking for me in a Goodwill in Roberts Junction. Believe me it is a good hiding place. I know you have a husband and children in Roberts Junction, but live and don't hide. If you have a dream, go for it. Don't hide like me. After this, I will make some changes in my life. I must go for it."

"Jamie, you are exactly right," Linda looked over at Robert and realized that she must go for it too. She had wasted too much time living a lie and not living the life she was born to live. Happy, giving and being loved. "I will try to call you again tomorrow. I don't have a cell phone for you to call me, but I think that will change very shortly."

"Yes, it must. Thanks again for calling and we shall talk soon."

"Yes, we shall," Linda hung up the phone.

Robert turned from the fire and said, "Everything okay?"

Linda said nothing because she was getting up from the couch, removing his t-shirt and headed to the floor to him all at the same time. He could clearly tell that this was her decision, her show and he didn't know what exactly she was about to do, but he knew that he was going to like it. The only words that came from Linda were, "It is time that I really start living, loving and leading my own life. Please lay down on your back sir." Robert put the poke back in the stand near the fire place. He laid on the pallet of blankets he created at the fire place stretching out his arms, hands and feet. By now, Linda straddled him completely naked. She kissed him thoroughly on the mouth and helped him removed his clothes one piece at a time. She kissed or licked every exposed inch of skin on him. He moaned and groaned loudly to show his distinct pleasure in her every touch. She massaged him from his feet and ankles all the way to his shoulders and head. She moved down over his body so that her face was clearly over his shaft and licked him from his groin to his tip. By the time she reached the top, he was totally erect, she was wet and ready to take him completely. She lowered her body on his taunt penis and brought his hands up to massage her breasts as she rode him to victory like Calvin Burrell on a Kentucky Derby Horse. James always made fun of her breasts, but Robert seemed to enjoy stroking and touching each one. He put each one in his mouth and sucked them like he was breast feeding. Little did Robert know that her breasts were small, but super sensitive. The sucking motion of Robert drove Linda clearly over the edge which made her ride him even harder and harder. When they came together, they both screamed. She laid her body on top of Robert's with her head gently on his chest. He caressed her head as he stroked her back. As their breathing returned to normal, he said, "I love you."

"Please don't say it if you don't mean it. I don't think I can bear to leave hearing you say that again and again."

"I love you and again I love you and that's all there is to it."

"Robert what am I going to do?"

"You are going to go back to Roberts Junction and make your decision. I have been waiting for you this long, I can wait a little while longer. It will nearly kill me, but you have to face it. If you want, I will gladly go with you. I can't make you stay if you don't want to. I made the decision years ago and didn't fight for you. Today, I am using the only two fighting tactics I know that work."

"What's that?"

"Love you so good that you can't leave or love you so good that you can't go away and stay."

"Oh, Robert," was all that Linda could say before she knew that she had to have him one more time. That pallet became their love bed for the next few hours. The hunger for each other superseded the hunger for food.

"R'etta, I think that it's time," he said.

"Time for what?" Ms. Henrietta asked.

"It's time that we stop hiding, pretending and tell everyone the truth," he added.

"Are you ready?" Ms. Henrietta inquired.

"Yes, I am ready. I think that we should move and live in Florida for the rest of our days. There is no sense hiding here in Roberts Junction. The kids will be happy to come and see us in Florida," he stated emphatically.

"Yes, Lord. I am so tired of this cold weather so if you are ready, I am," Ms. Henrietta said.

"John, how long has it been since you stayed in your house?" Grace asked quietly.

"At least six months," John and Grace had made many stops in the snow storm, but were now safe and sound back at John's house. John had a lovely one-story house with three bedrooms and two bathrooms. There was a basement unfinished with a washer and dryer and storage. He always needed a basement just in case of a tornado or other inclement weather. John put Grace's number in his phone first and that was all for now. He knew that he would put his mother's number in his phone soon, but he right now he was in a rebellious mood.

"What do you want me to help you do?"

"Well, I need to get some heat on, build a fire in the fireplace and get something to eat in you."

"I'll start dinner while you work on the fireplace. I don't know where anything is, but I know how to open cabinets," Grace giggled as she opened each cabinet to find something new or to find nothing. John had a lot of things to purchase and would take his time getting those things.

"It's a deal," John and Grace moved about his house with ease. Grace noticed that John had a small boom box on the counter so she turned it on. Fortunately, it was set to smooth jazz which was Grace's favorite. There was not much to fix because they got one of those already cooked rotisserie chickens, some mixed vegetables, baked potatoes and rolls. John came back in the kitchen, but stopped short in the doorway and nearly cried seeing the sight of a woman in his kitchen. He was overwhelmed by the idea, but seeing it for himself was incredible. Grace was swaying her hips to the beat of the music as she stirred the vegetables. John creeped up behind her and wrapped his arms around her waist turning her into his arms for one twirl around the kitchen make-shift dance floor. The spoon was still in Grace's hands, but she didn't seem to mind.

"Oh, John, you startled me. I didn't realize that you were standing there. I thought you were still in the living room."

"I didn't mean to startle you, but I just wanted to join in the dance without interrupting you. Standing there watching you dancing in my kitchen made me want to dance with you right then and there." Their height difference was clearly noticeable. She was only five foot three and John stood at least six foot two inches tall.

"I love music. I usually have music playing in the background all over the house."

"Thank you for everything today."

"For what?"

"Today was quite a traumatic moment in my life. You were there to help me through it, and thank you again," John was still swaying to the music and looking into Grace's eyes.

"You are welcome, again," Grace held John's gaze, but remembered the vegetables on the stove. "I better check on the veggies before they burn." Grace returned to the stove, and John set the table. "The veggies are ready. We can go ahead and eat," Grace said. John took Grace's hand and said a prayer over the food.

"God, thank you for this food and Grace. Help us to move forward with our lives together. Amen."

"Amen."

"You've already shared something very personal with me. I feel like we are doing this relationship in reverse, but somehow it feels so right. Is there something personal you want to share with me?" John asked.

"I know. It's weird and I must tell you this. My ex-husband's mother told him to divorce me. I think that is the main reason why I said what I said to your mother. I haven't told you what I do for a living. I am a librarian. I needed to go back to school to get my Master's Degree in Library Science. The only library schools back then were IU in Bloomington and University of Kentucky in Lexington. I didn't want to commute. I wanted to live on campus so I could get finished quicker and he worked manual labor jobs then finishing his degree in Forensic Science. I thought he could get a job in either one of those places quickly and finish his degree as well. Our daughter wasn't born then so it would have been just the two of us. Two adults can eat

Ramen noodles every night without a baby. His mother said we should settle down and raise a family and not try to reach too high with advanced degrees. Wasn't one degree enough? My undergraduate degree is in Business. Also, that if we moved to Lexington or Bloomington, I would be taking him too far away from her so he divorced me."

"Wow, just for school?"

"Just for school."

"I don't know why I am surprised. My mother didn't want me to see you and we hadn't even been on our first date yet. So, who is your daughter's father?"

"My ex-husband."

"huh?"

"We met for a weekend in Bowling Green to try to reconcile. I got pregnant, but we didn't remarry because his mom told him not to. He was a very nice guy too, but not strong enough to say no to his mother."

"Do you think I am strong enough?" John asked as he put his fork down and looked at Grace across the table.

"When you didn't take your phone tonight from your mom's house, I knew that you were strong enough," Grace said sincerely.

"I could fall off the wagon."

"Yes, it could happen. You could call her right now too. You could walk out that door and drive back to her house and leave me here in this blizzard too."

"Yes, I could."

"But, you won't because you want your own life really bad and willing to fight for it. I hope it was easier for you to fight because I was with you. I was with my ex-husband too and he still did what his mother told him to and divorced me."

"Seriously. Do you think I will do that too?"

"I don't know, but I am willing to take the risk to find out. Shoot me 'cuz I am a sucker for a nice guy," John and Grace both chuckled and spent the rest of the evening finding out ways to solidify their relationship. The snow continued that evening well into the night. About a foot of snow fell in all. They were happily stuck in the house together revealing their past, stating their present and mapping out their future. Grace called to check in with her daughter and let her know that she was okay with a new friend. John never touched his new phone at all. One step towards total freedom.

Chapter 12 – Believe Me

Monday morning, I-65 highway was opened in both directions, north and south. Jamie called Steve and told him about her parents dying and that she would need the rest of the week off for an emergency. Steve said no problem at all. Jamie caught the *Greyhound* bus from downtown Roberts Junction, IN to Indianapolis, IN to finish the arrangements for her parents' burial and to settle their estate matters. The schools were closed as well as most of the businesses in Roberts Junction, because the hills and narrow roads were too dangerous for school buses to go across and cars for that matter except emergency vehicles. Grace was off from work. John took off from work at the Goodwill for several reasons. First, he realized that he was working more to get away from his mother. Second, it was impolite to leave a guest in your home especially when you wanted to continue making love to them all day until utter exhaustion. Finally, he decided that he and Grace needed more time for discovery, revelation and planning for their future.

James went to work as usual because office managers don't need a real day off especially when they play all day where they work. The female employees of Sanders and Associates wished James would take off more so that he would leave them alone.

Steve didn't open up the Goodwill at all because all of his employees were out of town. They all needed one more day to get themselves together. He didn't need to go to the store to put a sign on the door, because if anybody was crazy enough to come to the store, they would see that it was closed.

Ms. Henrietta wasn't going anywhere anytime soon and especially not on Monday because that was her usual day off and her bones didn't move too well on Mondays after church on Sunday.

Robert Matthews owned Matthews & Associates so he called his secretary and said that he was unavailable to anyone who didn't have an emergency or his cell number. She was instructed not to give his number to anyone that wasn't worth at least eight figures or had an emergency that couldn't wait until Tuesday. In his words, "most of the Midwest was covered in snow so everybody should be safe in their homes and not messing with anybody enough to sue right now." While Robert was on the phone with his secretary, Linda rolled over to the other side of the bed and checked on her kids again. They were both safe and sound at the Parkers' house. This time she talked with Ryan's mother, and she assured Linda that her sons were nothing but real gentlemen and welcomed in her home anytime. She had enough food because Ryan ate enough for three people by himself so they were fine. She also let Linda know that they wouldn't let Ryan drive back to school until the highway was safe for a 21-year-old to drive on it. Indiana University was closed for the day, and they weren't going to be missing class anyway. Maybe they would try to let the boys go back on Tuesday morning but definitely not driving at night. With her mind at ease about her kids, Linda rolled back over in bed toward Robert until he hung up the phone to find that mole that he said he had since high school that she missed on their last round of discovery.

Jamie's bus arrived in Indianapolis at 1:00 p.m. sharp. David knew that he would recognize Jamie immediately, but didn't know whether she would recognize him. As soon as Jamie walked into the bus station with her small, David walked up to her and said, "Jamie, it's me David." Jamie blinked because he said his name was David, but she could have sworn he looked just like her ex-boyfriend from high school Jeremy.

"Jeremy?"

"Yes, it's me. I go by David now."

"Why didn't you tell me?"

"Two reasons. You have been to emotional hell and back.
Next, you might not believe me so I wanted you to see me in
person."

"Oh, my goodness, it has been at least 15 years since I have
seen you. What have you been doing with your life?"

"I will tell you everything once we get in the car. Are you
hungry?"

"Yes, I am starving, but I can't eat anything until after I have
gone to the funeral home and taken care of business. I just
might throw up."

"I understand," David or the boy that she once knew as
Jeremy Noles, led her to a black Jeep Cherokee truck and put
her bag in the back and opened the passenger car door for
her. Jamie had dressed in one of her few dressy outfits. Most
of her dressy clothes she didn't wear any more since she
worked in a Goodwill store and hadn't had a date in five
years. Today, it was a black pantsuit with a bright yellow
turtleneck and high heeled boots. The long black top coat
kept Jamie warm in this fierce winter. She knew that this

was a special, unhappy time in her life and that she should dress the part. David headed the car toward the funeral home to finish making the arrangements. Jamie remembered a very nice, tall, smooth faced boy who had a little wild streak. The person that just put her in the car was a grown ass, gorgeous man.

"Okay, so tell me about yourself, and what's been going on with you."

"Why don't we handle business first, and then I will tell you all you need to know over dinner."

"Cool. My co-workers always tell me that I am nosy Jamie and just meddle into everybody else's business. To be honest, it is a cover. I don't want to deal with my own business. This has been even harder because I have so much regret."

"I know that it is very hard for you. I am here to help you face everything. I am your representative from Matthews & Associates to take care of your parents' estate matters. Furthermore, I am your friend."

"Wow, I don't deserve it but, I thank you Jeremy or is it, David? What name are you going by?"

"David. The name Jeremy had so many bad memories of where I came from and the place I never want to return, that I go by my middle name, David which keeps me moving forward."

"Exactly. I need to get a map to find out where 'moving forward' is right now."

"You will figure it out. It will take time but the forward map will come," David drove in silence to allow Jamie to prepare herself and take in the change of the Indianapolis landscape. There was so much new development that someone who had been away from the city for many years would get lost. David watched as Jamie's eyes lit up like a kid going to the circus while taking in the new sights of the city.

Jamie and David were greeted by the funeral director when they arrived at the funeral home. Jamie didn't attend many funerals. If she could avoid it at all costs, she would. Burying both of her parents is something that she never dreamed would happen. Thank goodness for David. He was familiar, her parents' lawyer and a support system that she never expected. David did as he said and guided her through every step at the funeral home including the legal and some preferences of her parents' that Jamie had no knowledge of.

Jamie's parents had prepaid and arranged for everything from the service to the burial. The main thing that Jamie needed to do was sign and approve the small stack of paperwork. The entire process took nearly one hour and a half to get it all done. The announcement would be in tomorrow's paper and the memorial service would be on Wednesday at the mausoleum chapel. Whoever showed up would show up.

When David and Jamie left the funeral home, he asked, "Jamie are you ready to eat, or do you need to go to the house first?"

"No, I am not ready for the house yet. I need some food and maybe even a stiff drink to get me through it."

"Whatever you want. I am here for you."

"Thank you."

David moved quickly through the streets of Indianapolis back downtown to the Yard House on Maryland for an intimate late lunch/early dinner. Jamie didn't cry throughout the process, but David could tell that she was physically and emotionally worn out. The sooner they got through this lunch/dinner the quicker she could get some rest. David had brought a few dates here, but mostly clients to relax over drinks and good food. The one person that he always wanted to bring to the Yard House was finally sitting across from him, Jamie Miller.

"Are you now ready to tell me how you got from that trailer park to the nice cars, fancy restaurants and a big title job?"

"Well, that night we got caught having sex on my truck changed me."

"Oh no! I will never forget that as long as I live."

"Exactly. To me, I was on cloud nine and thought the night was going great until the bright lights and sirens. The officer wasn't nice to me or thought I was worth much. Clearly your parents agreed with the officer, especially your father. I can still hear him say, 'You let a Noles put his dick in you?' I decided that very night to make something of myself. It didn't matter what it took. I was going to be somebody one day."

"I am so sorry for what my father said. I don't think I really took up for you that night as I should."

"Well, what were you supposed to say and still live under his roof?"

"Really."

"The way I remember it we both sat on that couch and said nothing."

"Exactly. At that time, there was no talking while my daddy was talking. I thought I was big and bad, but I still respected my dad. On the other hand, I was rebellious enough until I got caught. I should have said something."

"No, problem. That was so long ago that I have not forgotten, but forgiven you for any hurt I felt that day. Those words of your father's were the fuel that moved my mission possible bus to where I am today. I was going to prove to them that I was worth something, but I was also going to prove it to you too."

"I didn't get to stay around to see you really rise to prominence because I got in so much trouble that they put me on a bus and that's how I landed in Roberts Junction."

"I saw the trial and all of the publicity that went along with it. I am sorry that you ended up with a creep like that."

"It was my own doing. I had to learn a hard lesson. When you are a young thrill seeker and actually find what you are seeking, but it can turn out to be hell instead of thrilling. The trap is shut and you have to fight your way out."

"I understand because I have seen enough guys from the trailer park end of up in jail and some I have defended. They tell me how smart I am now, but they called me a geek, 'book worm' and other oh so not nice names while I was getting my education."

"So how did you turn everything around to get into law school?"

"When you broke up with me after that wonderful/horrible night, I brought my grades up, stopped hanging out with the crazy trailer park bunch and started going around the library club bunch. I suffered a lot of ridicule for it. I couldn't let any of that stop me though, because I was on a mission and had a plan. My plan was to make your parents respect me and hopefully get you to go out with me again."

"For real?"

"For real. Just to let you know, that 'Jeremy it's not you it's me' speech that I first heard from you, I heard another hundred times. I am the nice guy that grew up on the wrong side of the tracks. I wasn't 'bad boy' enough to get the homecoming queen or the girl next door."

"Yuck. I am sorry for everything. For the way things turned out for you, it was probably good that we did break up. I was not living in the trailer park or hanging out with that crew, but my head wasn't wrapped up too tight."

"You were young and things happen when you are young."

"You're right," Just then their server came to the table with their food. They changed to a lighter subject. David knew that there would be a flood of new emotions when Jamie arrived at her parents' house. He had plenty of time this week to ask her about her time in Roberts Junction, was she seeing anyone and what her plans were for the future.

Jamie had so many thoughts going on in her head and body that she couldn't focus on anything besides the death of her parents and the irony of reconnecting with Mr. Jeremy David Noles. They finished their meal, returned to the car, and in silence, they headed toward the next hurdle in Jamie's journey, the house. Jamie had not been back to the house for any holiday, birthday, Mother's or Father's Days since that day they put her on the bus headed away from Indianapolis. David stopped the car in front of the house and said nothing. He took his cues strictly from Jamie. He remembered coming back to this house for the first time after that wonderful/horrible night with Jamie and the quite different treatment he experienced when he accompanied Robert Matthews to discuss the Millers' estate. Mr. Miller hadn't recognized David Noles at first but soon asked whether he knew a Jeremy Noles. David answered as only he could, "I am Jeremy Noles, sir. I go by David Noles which is my middle name." Mr. Miller was surprised and admitted that the last time that he had seen him he wouldn't have expected him to be a lawyer or any type of respectable citizen in the community. David told Mr. Miller that it was because of that last night in this very home that completely changed his life. David didn't mention Jamie and neither did the Millers. It was a very emotional day for David too. Sitting in the car with Jamie now, he still remembered every detail vividly. David took Jamie's hand but still said nothing. Jamie took a deep breath, gently squeezed David's hand to reassure him and opened the car door. David had the keys to the house. When he opened the door, all of the furniture was still in the same place as she remembered more than fifteen years earlier. As soon as she crossed the threshold of the house, she broke down and cried interchanging and alternating between screams and gulps of air. David put an arm around her shoulders, she turned into his arms, encircled in a full embrace with her head resting on his chest. He was only a few inches taller than Jamie, but her head fit perfectly under his chin. Jamie regained her composure and began to walk around the house.

Even though Jamie was an only child, the Millers' house was huge. There were five bedrooms, six baths and three levels and a full finished basement with a theatre, an enclosed swimming pool for year-round swimming. Tennis courts were in the back of the house. It was large when Jamie lived there, but had full-time servants who lived on the place 3 days a week for the upkeep. It seemed overwhelmingly large without her parents or anyone staying in the house.

"I'm sorry," Jamie said quietly. Her voice still echoed throughout the house.

"Stop saying that you are sorry. I understand," David said to reassure her.

"Stop saying that you understand! How could you?" Jamie was yelling at David through her pain and hurt.

"I do understand! My father was killed by a drunk driver more than five years ago!" David yelled back.

"I'm sorry I didn't know," Jamie covered her mouth with her hand like David had just slapped her. Jamie walked over to David to hug and comfort him.

"I know you didn't know but, it's true. My dad was drunk himself so really both drivers were drunk and killed each other. The forensics report said that the other car crossed the line first which caused the accident. So, I do know what it's like to lose a father to a drunk driver, but I was in communication with my dad before he died, you were not. I don't know what that feels like."

"Be grateful that you don't. Some of it is pride mixed with pain mixed with more pride and topped with embarrassment and shame. I have a request. I don't deserve to ask, but there is no one in this city to call."

"Anything."

"Can you stay in one of the other bedrooms tonight? This house is too large for me to stay in alone."

"Fine with me, but I have to let Robert know and arrange my schedule for tomorrow."

"Thank you."

"Do you realize that I have been in this house for three days and haven't put on a bra yet?" Robert and Linda were in his bedroom watching television fresh out of the shower with matching t-shirts from his closet.

"No offense but you don't really need to. You are one of the few women in the world that could go bra-less and it would be okay," Linda hit Robert slightly on the arm for that teasing remark.

Robert pretended to be hurt, "Ouch."

"Hey, now. I thought about having a breast enlargement."

"Why?"

"Because they are so small."

"Yes, but wouldn't you lose the sensitivity in them if they were enlarged?"

"Yes, I guess."

"Don't do it. I love them just like they are. They fit nicely in the palm of my hands, and the way you react to them in my mouth gets me aroused just thinking about it."

"Don't start nothing you can't finish."

"Oh, I can start it, keep it going and finish it, beautiful lady," Linda giggled at the thought of making love to Robert. The past three days had been a sexual fantasy, dream, pleasure and marathon all in one. She was twenty years overdue. She and Robert had been making up for a lot of lost time. As much as she would like to indulge, she knew that she had to stop everything and once again broach the subject.

"Now, before you get started and ultimately finish, I have to talk it through, okay?"

"Okay. You can talk to me about anything. What is it?"

"I know that you said the choice was left up to me, but James is mean, cruel and harsh. He is not going to let me go easily.

I don't know how long I am going to be in Roberts Junction before we can really be together."

"Take as long as you must. I'll be waiting. I have told you that over and over again. I was going to give this to you later, but now seems like the right time," Robert leaned over to his night stand on his side of the bed and pulled out a box. Linda wondered what was in the box but realized that it was bigger than a ring box and her breath returned to normal.

"Here take this."

"What is it?" Linda took the lid off of the box as Robert continued to explain.

"It's a phone. No one has the number but me. I made sure that the number was not listed in any directory. If you need me, you only have to press 1 and this green button which is the send. If he acts like he is getting ready to hit or harm one hair on your beautiful head, call me. I will have him in custody so fast, it will make his head spin. I have no love for or tolerance with any abusive man to a woman. If a man tried to harm my daughter or anything else I loved and that includes you or anything you love, I would kill him. Linda, I am so serious about this I will stake my life on it. Look at me. I love you now, I have always loved you and always will love you. Don't think for one minute that I would blow this one chance that I have to fix things between us. I have waited, prayed and worked too hard to blow this chance with you. I want to love and take care of you for the rest of your life. You will never have to work another day in your life if you don't want to. I am here to fulfill all of your dreams, fantasies and your heart's desire too. I have had many opportunities to marry the wrong person, but I waited and thank God that I did."

"Oh Robert, I don't deserve you. I am not free to love you as you should be loved. If you will give me a little time to get things together with my sons, I will try my best to love you the way you have showed me that a person should be loved."

"Don't try, just do it. If this weekend is any indicator of the love that you are capable of Linda, I may need to go see a heart doctor. You are the most passionate woman I know," Linda giggled at the thought of how uninhibited she had been the entire weekend.

"I must admit, I have embarrassed myself. I can truthfully say that you bring it out of me."

"Happy to be on the receiving end of so much passion. It's been a long time for me and it was worth the wait."

"Me too, me too," Linda put the phone and box on the night stand. She went easily into the safety of Robert's arms as she had all weekend. Linda realized that safety, security and serenity in a relationship was most important to her now and not money. Tomorrow she would go and face James. This would be the fight of her life, but she only had one life to live. Why should she not live her life to the fullest with someone who really loved and cared about her?

Tuesday was a turning point on so many levels for the entire community of Roberts Junction. People were busy digging out from the foot and a half of snow that blanketed the ground. The hardware store was all a buzz with getting shovels, salt and deicer for windows and doors to get back to normal in the town. The highway was open and so were most of the businesses in Roberts Junction. William and Ryan headed out early to get back before Ryan's 9:00 a.m. class. Ryan called his parents as soon as they arrived on campus to let them know that they were back safely. The Goodwill was open too. This morning, John was the first to arrive at the Goodwill and was feeling fully awake and alive. John figured that Linda would arrive late because she had been out of town all weekend. So, John went to Steve's house and got the keys to open the door. Steve wasn't due into the store until noon. John finally had let Grace go back to her house on Monday evening, after much trepidation and longing. John remembered saying multiple times, "Just a few more minutes, one more kiss, don't go just yet or I miss you already." It had been a long time since either were in a relationship so the newness of it was wonderfully fresh. Linda came next to the store after it had been opened an hour. She had gotten out of her car and ran back in the house to Robert so many times that she was late arriving even though she was dressed, had eaten breakfast and the car was packed at 6:30 a.m. Linda had felt trapped in a loveless relationship so long that to feel, see and experience a love so genuine was so very hard to leave. Like John it took Linda multiple tries to leave Robert in Bloomington and come back to Roberts Junction. When she came in, there was nobody in the front part of the store.

"Hello!" Linda called out.

"Hello!" John called out from the storage room back to her.

"Hey, John, are you the only one in the store?"

"Yep, it's just me. There have been no customers yet this morning, so we are fine. Steve told me that Jamie's parents were killed in a drunk driving accident, and she won't be in the rest of the week."

"Yes, I talked to her on Sunday and she is still in shock, I think. It took a little longer to get out of Bloomington than expected," Of course, Linda couldn't tell John that she was making love to Robert one more time, on his kitchen floor with the syrup from the waffles being licked off of his chest.

"That is awful. You were out of town; how did you know about Jamie since you have been out of town?"

"A mutual attorney friend told me," Linda didn't want to think about their mutual friend right now. Linda had called Robert when she got to Roberts Junction to let him know that she had arrived safe and sound. Robert was almost to Indianapolis to resume his work as well. She had promised him that she would let him know how things went with James. Her biggest worry was telling James that she wanted out of this relationship.

"Well, since we are alone, I want to let you know that I moved out of my mom's house and spent the weekend with a wonderful young lady at my house this weekend."

"What? How do you go from your mom's house, to your house and spending the weekend with a woman so fast?"

"To make a long story short. I met Grace in the grocery store on Friday morning and she had her grandson with her. She later had an accident right in front of my mom's house and slid into the ditch on Saturday around noon. My mom could tell that we had a great chemistry, and she bawled Grace out. The only problem is that I heard my mom. She tried to manipulate me for the last time, and I left."

"Good for you. So how is it going with Grace, is that her name?"

"Yes, she is Grace. It's going fantastic. I have had so much love to give and my mom was keeping me from it, because she wanted me all to herself which is weird. I didn't see it at first, but now I do. How was your weekend?"

"Well, you know Indiana lost the game."

"Yes, I did see that much on the news."

"Look at all this stuff piled up. The other stuff that happened would take all day to explain. So, I will tell you another day. I am late and we've got so much work to get done."

"You are right," Linda was thankful that John wouldn't press her for an explanation but, just went right to work. There was only two of them receiving merchandise, sorting and, working the floor and taking care of the cash register until Steve and Ms. Henrietta came in around noon.

An hour or so later, Steve and Ms. Henrietta came into the store. Ms. Henrietta was fussing about the cold and Steve said nothing. There wasn't a lot of business going on, so they were able to get the storage and receiving room in order so they wouldn't be too behind without Jamie. It was almost closing time and time for Linda to face the music and go home. She stayed until 5:30, because she arrived late and needed to get in all of her hours for the day.

Chapter 13 - Reality

Linda drove straight home. When she opened the door, she realized that James hadn't done anything in the kitchen all weekend. There were boxes, bags and empty containers from various fast-food restaurants, pots, pans and glasses placed everywhere. Things hadn't changed. James still thought he had a maid and he wasn't supposed to help do anything in the house. She didn't demand that he help so he didn't. 'No need to complain just need to get a trash bag and get started,' Linda thought. James' car wasn't in the garage so she had no clue when he would be home. She heard footsteps on the staircase and thought it was Stephen. Linda realized it was James by his yawn as he got to the bottom of the stairs. She braced herself, looked up and said, "Hello."

"So, you finally decided to bring your ass home?" Linda didn't respond right away but let that remark go by without a response.

"Where is your car? I didn't see it in the garage," she said as she went back to cleaning.

"I guess the bank came and picked it up," James said as he opened up the refrigerator door.

"Came and picked it up? What happened?" Linda stood looking at the back of his head and those god-awful shorts.

"I came out of the firm and it was not in my parking space. I guess I got behind on my payments and they came and repossessed it. I was going to pay them next month or so," James said while opening up a beer.

"You guess you got behind or you know you got behind in your payments?"

"Listen bitch, I have been under a lot of stress lately and forgot to pay it."

"How did you forget to pay it? I thought it takes several payments before they come and pick up your car. Right? Well, did you make the house payment?"

"Listen woman don't be confronting me about bills. I handle stuff around here. Your little Goodwill money you make don't pay for shit in this house."

"James, I don't know how much more of this I can take."

"How much more of what you don't think that you can take?"

"You don't want to be with me. You don't love me. I don't know why we are together," Linda said.

"I know why. Because your boyfriend Robert dumped you for 'good looks' Brooks and you got pregnant by me."

"Shut up!" Linda said.

James walked over to Linda and grabbed her around her throat. This was the first time that he had ever laid a hand on her that way. He proceeded to choke the life out of Linda. Linda grabbed both of his hands and dug her short nails into his skin to hurt him enough to let her go. James was spitting out, "Who you saying shut up to? I will kill you woman before you will disrespect me. You should be grateful that anybody looked your way."

"Dad! No! Let Mom go!" Stephen ran into the house just in time to stop James from squeezing the breath out of Linda's body. Stephen wedged his body in between his mom and dad causing James to finally let go. Linda didn't pass out but was gasping for air as she fell to the kitchen floor.

"Mom, are you okay?" Stephen helped his mother up off of the floor.

"I'll be fine son, thank you," Linda moved to the opposite end of the kitchen to get as far away from James as possible. Stephen still stood in close proximity to his father with his back to his mother for protection.

"I am sorry, I just got a little carried away. I didn't mean anything by it. I just had a bad day son and your mom got smart with me is all. It won't happen again," James quickly explained.

"I know it won't happen again because you are leaving," Stephen was the youngest, but he was bold and taking charge.

"Who are you to tell me what to do?" James asked. Stephen was nearly eighteen years old and only one inch shorter than his father. Stephen could easily look his father directly in the face.

"I am the one who is going to call the police in about 5 seconds if you don't get your stuff and get out of here," Stephen continued not backing down.

"I don't have a car son. That's what happened today. They came and repossessed it, and I don't have any transportation until I can pay. It is a blizzard outside."

"Dad, I don't care where you go, you have got to leave here," Stephen stood his ground.

"Who's going to make me?" James issued a challenge.

"Me and these pictures from this weekend?" Stephen opened his phone to the pictures.

"What pictures from this weekend?" Linda asked.

"These pictures!" Stephen put the phone in his father's face and revealed that he had taken pictures of the leftover food and utensils in the kitchen. There were images of Candy and James' clothes thrown all over the floor in the living room as well as vivid pictures of them in the bed upstairs.

"Those pictures don't mean anything."

"Yes. they do in a divorce court. I asked Ryan's father already. He said that in a settlement they mean a lot," Stephen stated.

James grabbed the phone out of Stephen's hands and slammed the phone against the wall. The phone shattered. James smiled at Stephen, "Now where are those pictures?"

"Backed up on my Google Plus account and in the cloud. I have everything on my phone automatically backed up. Dad, you bought the package for me."

"Well, I will cancel it, and you will lose all of those pictures."

"William and I have been paying our own phone bills for a while now, since you stopped paying the bill. You can't cut us off."

Suddenly, the front doorbell rang and James walked the few feet to open the door. There were two officers along with another well-dressed man on the other side of the screen door. "Yes?" James asked.

"Mr. James Sanders." Stephen and Linda moved into the living room to hear what the gentleman wanted with James.

"Yes, I am Mr. James Sanders."

"We have a warrant for your arrest."

"What the hell for!" James yelled.

"Rape of a minor."

"Raping who?"

"Ms. Candice Merriweather."

"Candice is a minor?"

"Yes, she is only seventeen years old. She is charging you with rape, sodomy and kidnapping because you picked her up a few blocks from her school on Friday and she remained in your home more than 24 hours."

"What the hell? This is some type of mistake. I don't know Candice Merriweather."

The one officer handcuffed James and said, "We'll get it all straightened out at the station sir, come quietly." The other one read him his rights. He was led down the steps, and they put him inside a police car.

James called back, "Linda, call my dad and tell him to come to the police station immediately and get me out!" Fortunately, it was late, dark outside and James went with the officers quietly, there was not too much of a scene or disturbance with the neighbors.

Linda stood there stunned and didn't say anything. She was still massaging her neck from James nearly choking her to death. Her brain was scrambled from everything that happened that day, "Stephen, you have been so brave and taking charge of everything. What do you think we should do next?"

"I think we need a lawyer. I also think we need to go to Ryan's parents' house, explain to them what happened and stay there tonight just in case grandpa gets Dad out. If Dad gets out, he will come back and try to kill both of us."

"I already have a lawyer, and son, you are probably right. My bags are still in the car. I just need fresh clothes. You go pack your bag while I make this call." Stephen went upstairs to pack a bag. He called his brother and filled him in on what happened. William told Stephen to stay close by their mother and continue to protect her from their father.

Linda picked her new phone out of her purse and pressed 1 and the send button like Robert had showed her earlier that day.

"Hello. Are you alright?" Robert answered on the first ring.

"Yes and no."

"What happened, and don't leave out anything. I have been worried sick all day. Do I need to come there tonight?"

"No, Robert, stay there in Indianapolis. I love your concern but listen first and then advise me on what to do. When I came home, James was already here. His car wasn't in the garage because it was repossessed. I didn't know he had any money issues. He always kept everything so private. Anyway, he was being mean to me as usual and I asked about the car, bills and why the car got repossessed. He insulted me. I finally got mad and yelled shut up back to him. He got mad when I stood up to him and yelled back, he grabbed me by the throat and began choking me. Stephen came in just in time and stopped him. I fell to the floor gasping for breath. I am alright."

"Choke you! I will kill him!" Robert interrupted and began stomping around his office like a caged animal.

"No, stop, listen. Love, please calm down."

Robert immediately lost all steam when she said, 'love.' "Say that again."

"Which part?"

"Love."

"Love, please calm down."

"You know I love you, but it is good to hear you call me that in return."

"It's so soon, but I think I am falling."

"I'll catch you."

"Please hold me tight," Linda paused because Robert's voice was causing her stomach to do flip flops and she wanted to be in his arms right then and there. "You're getting me off focus from my story."

"Okay, I am sorry."

"I'm not."

"Me either really, but go ahead."

"After he let me go, Stephen said that James must leave because he had some pictures from this past weekend. I didn't see the pictures because James grabbed the phone from Stephen, slammed the phone on the floor so hard it broke. Stephen told him that the pictures were backed up somewhere in the cloud. Where that is I don't know."

"You have a smart son."

"Thank you. Then the doorbell rang, and it was two police officers and I guess a detective at the door. They arrested James for raping a girl, seventeen years old."

"What?"

"Yes. James yelled back for me to come and bail him out of jail. That's it. I'm now on the phone with you."

"I'm just glad that you are safe. You are not going to spend a dime of your money getting him out of anywhere. You are going to let his ass rot in that jail. You do need to get to safety just in case his dad gets him out."

"That's what Stephen said. We are packing a bag now to go to a neighbor's house."

"Give me until tomorrow afternoon to get back to Roberts Junction. Jamie's parents' memorial service is tomorrow at noon and then I will come directly to you. I know that we haven't made any plans, but I think that I need to meet with you, your sons and discuss our next steps. Baby, don't worry about anything just get to safety and we will work everything out tomorrow."

"Thank you."

"You are welcome. I love you and can't wait until I see you on tomorrow. Good night."

"Good night to you too." Linda hung up the phone and thought 'I think I love him too.'

Stephen came down the steps with a bag in his hand, "Mom was that the lawyer and when did you get a phone?"

"Yes, that was the lawyer and I got a phone this weekend."

"Great. Mom, let's go and we can talk about everything else later." Linda and Stephen got in her car and drove to Ryan's parents' home and told them the whole story. Ryan's father, also a lawyer said that he would gladly help Robert with her case as well. Linda really had two lawyers which was even better. Linda went from having one jerk of a husband to having two very efficient lawyers willing to fight for her. She and Stephen were safe and that was all that mattered.

James was yelling from the holding cell, "Hey, hey, I know my rights. I at least get one phone call!!"

"Yes, you get one phone call. Make that phone call."

James dialed the number to his dad's cell phone, and it rang twice before he picked it up, "Hello."

"Dad, this is James."

"Where are you? The caller id says Department of Corrections. Are you locked up, Son?"

"Yes, Dad. I need you to come and get me out."

"What have you done son?"

"Nothing Dad, I haven't done nothing. They have me on some trumped-up charges of raping a minor, but I didn't know she was a minor. I need you to come and get me out."

"Does Linda know this?"

"Yes, they embarrassed me and arrested me at my house, in front of my wife and Stephen. I have got to get out."

"I knew that this day was going to come. Your mother and I have spoiled you rotten, and you have now finally gotten caught in something terrible. I tried to warn your mom to stop babying you and let you grow up but, you both wouldn't listen. Well, now it is time for you to start taking responsibility for your actions."

"I have taken responsibility for my actions and will take more responsibility when I get out of this jail. Please, Dad how soon can you come and bail me out."

"Never."

"Never!"

"Never, Son. From the looks of these pictures that were sent to me from Stephen's cell phone, the young woman has a case. You may be gone for quite a while. I am not going to post bail, save you and get you off any more. With rape charges, you are not getting out until there is a trial. You will have plenty of time in jail to think about your actions, devise a plan of how you will, if ever, make a living for yourself when you get out. I am through covering for you, overlooking your terrible habits and defending you against all of the female employees at our firm. No matter if you got Linda pregnant or not, she has been a good wife to you, gave you two wonderful sons that I pray don't grow up like you. You blew it! A seventeen-year-old girl, James, have you lost your mind! I will try to explain it all to your mother, but I am quite sure that she will try to defend you again. I will prosecute you myself before I let her get you out of this trouble. Stop being a baby and grow up! Enjoy the rest of the holidays in jail. Goodbye."

"No, Dad, please wait!!" James yelled through the pay phone, and then it went dead. All James heard on the other end of the line was that horrific dial tone. "I need one more call!" He demanded, but it was denied. James was returned to his cell.

Harold Sanders realized that he had done the hardest thing that he would ever do and that is turn his back on his son. Tough love is hard, but he had finally had enough. His next step would be life changing for him, his family and the firm.

"Robert, this is Harold Sanders."

"Hello, Harold what can I do for you?"

"Robert, I need to discuss some business with you."

"Alright, when do you need to meet?"

"As soon as possible."

"I should be down your way handling some other business tomorrow afternoon. Do you want to meet first thing Thursday morning?"

"Yes, how about 10:00 a.m.? Is that fine with you?"

"I will meet you in your office at 10:00 a.m."

"See you then."

"Goodbye."

Robert knew that this trip to Roberts Junction was the most important of his life. Robert called David, his associate.

"Hello."

"Hello, David."

"Yes, sir."

"How are things going with Jamie?"

"As well as to be expected. She is going through the house and trying to figure out her next steps. I have advised her not to do anything, but just wait until all of the emotions of tomorrow are done and then make decisions in a week or so."

"Is she going to stay in Indianapolis the rest of the week or coming back to Roberts Junction?"

"She said that she wants to go back to Roberts Junction right after the memorial service. I have worked here all day via phone and laptop. I am headed to my house in a few minutes to pack a bag. She asked me to stay here tonight so we can leave together after the service."

"Well, when you pack that bag, make sure that you plan to stay the rest of the week. I will be there the rest of the week myself. I have a meeting with Harold Sanders on Thursday morning. My plans for myself have changed, and I think my plans for you in Roberts Junction may have changed as well. The woman that I was with this weekend is Linda Sanders, the daughter in law of Harold Sanders. Without going into much detail, I am in love with Linda. She has a lot that needs to be worked out. I am committed to helping her. The Indianapolis office runs like a well-oiled machine and if there are any emergencies, they can call us and/or handle it. I will make sure that Bruce or Lori is up to speed on what's going on with us while we are in Roberts Junction. I will see you at the memorial service tomorrow at noon."

"See you then and good night." Robert finished all of his tasks at the office and headed to his house after a long emotional day. He wanted to check on Linda again before he would be able to get any sleep.

Linda was at the Parkers' house discussing the situation hoping and praying that everything would work out alright. They bid her good night and told her that she could stay as long as she needed to. Linda assured them that she hoped that they could return to their house tomorrow. She thanked them again and again for allowing her and Stephen to stay as well as keeping Stephen and William in their home while she was out of town. Tomorrow, she needed to get him to school, replace Stephen's phone and plan the rest of her life.

The phone rang on the night stand and Linda knew who that was. Just like when she dated Robert in high school, he always called before he went to sleep. She got under the covers just as she pressed the button to answer.

"Hello."

"Hey, beautiful. I am missing you. How are things now?"

"Missing you too. Things are okay. I am at the neighbors' house and in bed about to go to sleep at the sound of your voice. I wish you were here."

"Me too but I will be there tomorrow. I have to tell you something. I told you that I was going to Sanders & Associates last week when I saw you right?"

"Right."

"I saw James first, and then I went to talk to his father, Harold."

"Okay."

"Harold just called me and wants to meet with me on Thursday. I don't know exactly what he wants, but I wanted you to know that I am meeting with him. He told me on our last meeting that he was thinking about retiring. I just wanted you to know. Another thing, I don't know if this is the right time to tell you, but I don't want any secrets between us."

"What is it?" Linda sat up in the bed and was scared at what he would say next.

"When I went to visit James, I caught him in his office with one of the receptionists going down on him. They didn't lock the door and I walked right in."

"What?! So, he has been tormenting me for years. Now, I find out that he's been screwing around with the women in the office, out in the streets and now some young girl on the other side of town in our bed at the house!"

"I'm sorry, but I didn't want any of our relationship to be built on a lie or keeping secrets. After everything else, I didn't want to keep it from you."

"I am furious and feel like a stupid idiot. I am glad that you were honest with me. I realize now that I stayed because of the boys. At the time, I really didn't know what else to do."

"First, never say that you are stupid around me ever again. You are highly intelligent, but haven't had a chance and concentrated on other priorities. You will get that chance if I have anything to do about it. Second, you are not an idiot either. Third, if you listen to what people tell you long enough, you start to believe it. I don't fault you for wanting to stay for the boys and try to keep your family together, but I was always taught that it takes two. I wish I could shield and protect you from the harsh reality of James and what lies ahead in this process, but I can't. I just want to love and advise you so that you can move forward and, little by little, forget the past."

"I don't know what I did to deserve you."

Robert smiled and let a low breathy sigh that Linda could hear through the phone. He turned out his light and laid down on his bed.

"What you did was remain the angel that you are. Remember that you have rocked my world as well. I am trying hard not to think of all of the ways, positions and places that we've made love in this house."

Linda giggled and laid back down on the bed, "Don't remind me."

"This bed seems so big without you in it."

"Well, this bed is a small twin bed, but if you were here, I would get close enough to you to give you some room."

"Would you?"

"You better believe I would."

"Lady, you are going to keep me warm in my dreams tonight." Linda and Robert continued to pleasure each other via phone until they could stay awake no longer.

"You have a long day tomorrow so I had better let you go."

"I do have a long day tomorrow, but now that I have had you, I will never let you go."

"That is so sweet."

"That's me. Robert 'the sweetest' Matthews."

"Good night, love."

"Good night to you right back. Bye."

They hung up the phone and sleep came easily for them both.

Chapter 14 - Decisions

The next day in Indianapolis, there was a small crowd gathering in the chapel to pay their last respects to the Millers. Jamie was escorted and under the watchful eye of David. Robert Matthews arrived around 11:45.

"Hello, Ms. Miller. I am Robert Matthews. We have spoken on the phone, but I am glad to be with you today even under these circumstances. I am so sorry about the loss of your parents. I have known your parents for many years and was honored to help them with their estate planning."

"Thank you so much. Please call me Jamie. I had no idea that day in the Goodwill that you were my parents' attorney. I am sorry if I was in anyway unprofessional. I was only teasing and having fun with my good friend, Linda Sanders. David has taken great care of me and handling my business. I thank you and him for all of your help throughout this process."

"No problem. It was our pleasure. David tells me that you will probably be returning to Roberts Junction to make plans for your next move?" Robert asked.

"Yes, I am going back to Roberts Junction to make some hard decisions."

"I have business in Roberts Junction as well and will be leaving right after the service." Robert said.

"I am packed and have everything in the car to go back to Roberts Junction once we finish here as well. David tells me that you have instructed him to stay the week for some other business. I hope that we can meet around a meal while you both are in town," Jamie said.

"I hope that we can make that happen as well."

Just then the minister stood at the front of the chapel and began. "If we can all take our seats, we will begin." Robert left them both and sat in a seat near the exit. The service was beautiful, touching and lasted about 30 minutes. Robert headed out immediately when the minister said "Amen." Linda was on his mind and getting to her as fast as his car would go was his top priority.

The snow was gone, but it was still cold in Roberts Junction. Linda put on a turtle neck to hide the slightly purple ring around her neck from James' hand prints, and the *Tylenol* took care of the soreness. She had arrived at work on time today with a smile on her face because she knew that she would see Robert today. John was smiling as well, because he had spent another night with Grace.

Linda and the crew at the Goodwill worked steadily to make up for lost time and being short staffed. Robert had not called, but Linda knew he was on the way. She had a feeling that he would either stop by or call her as soon as he got to town. Linda wanted to go back to her house tonight and not wear out her welcome at the Parkers but her and Stephen's safety was paramount. Linda bought a new cell phone for Stephen and he was to stop by and pick it up after school. The sales associate had given her the new number and at least they would have clear communication to each other and William. James didn't have either of these numbers so they wouldn't have to worry about him calling.

When the bell rang on the door, Linda was working out on the sales floor and Stephen was walking toward her. "Hey, Mom."

"Hey baby, how was school today?"

"Fine. I found it hard to concentrate with everything else going on. I did my best."

"I know, but that will all be solved soon enough. It may get a little harder before it gets easier. Here is your phone. I don't know what all it does, but you will know by the time I see you later."

"Thanks, Mom. Jason and I will figure it out."

"I just wanted to let you know that my lawyer is on his way to Roberts Junction and I will probably meet him after work. I need to go by the house this evening as well to check the mail and pick up the newspaper from the box."

"Mom, be careful."

"Thanks so much for your concern. The lawyer will be with me so I'll be fine."

"Do I get to meet him? I am not a baby. I think I am old enough to know what's about to happen next with us. William and I have already discussed some things. We are going to support you in whatever decision you make. We are not babies, so you don't need to stay in a relationship that is not healthy for you or us. We love you most of all."

"Thank you, sweetie, for you and your brother's support. I have really worried about how you guys felt about everything."

"Mom, we decided that when we caught Dad on Saturday. No matter what, you don't deserve the way he has treated you."

"Thank you," Linda realized even more how lucky she was to have two of the best sons in the world. She wiped away a tear from her eye at the thought.

"Mom, don't cry."

"I can't help it," Stephen hugged his mom and her head landed in his chest. This was once Linda's baby in her arms, now he was big enough to wrap his arms around her and comfort her. "I am so very proud of you and your brother. In spite of it all."

"Jason is outside so I am headed back over to the Parkers."

"I will call you and let you know what my plans are after I talk to the attorney."

"Bye, Mom."

"Bye, baby."

Stephen looked back and smiled at his mom.

"Wow, that's Stephen? He is a nearly grown man," John commented as he watched the young man walk out of the store.

"Yes, he is."

"You are lucky that you have two great kids. That is one of my only regrets is that I let my mom delay me out having kids of my own. I don't mind a woman that has kids and grandkids, but I would have liked one or two of my own."

"Well, John with men you are never too old. Look at some of these celebrities out here with little kids and they are in their 60's and 70's."

"Yeah, but they have nannies, don't take care of their kids and just see them on weekends. I would have wanted to be hands on and attend ball games, school plays and carnivals. Now, I just want to retire and travel the world."

"You are right. How does your mom like Grace?"

"She doesn't like her at all, but she will come around. I haven't talked to her in four days. I think that is a record."

"Wow, proud of you."

The doorbell rang again and it was Robert. He was rushing through the aisles to see Linda but stopped short when he saw John.

They both said nothing so Linda looked up at Robert and broke the ice, "Hey."

"Hey." This one word was all that Robert could say at the moment. He was just glad to see Linda safe and sound.

"John, this is Robert Matthews," Linda said still looking directly in Robert's eyes.

"Yes, I remember you from last week," that's all John said as he walked away. Robert never took his eyes off of Linda. He just raised his hand slightly in acknowledgement.

"Linda, is there some place private we can talk," Robert finally found his voice and more words.

"Yes, in the back room," Linda said.

"Go ahead Linda, I got it," John didn't know all of the details, but from a distance and Robert's intense look at Linda, spoke volumes, "Steve nor Ms. Henrietta is here yet. If I need you, I will call you."

"Thanks, John." Linda and Robert headed to the back room.

As soon as the doors closed and they were out of sight, Robert reached for Linda. She went into arms gladly. They kissed and kissed until breathless.

"Oh God, I have missed you."

"Me too."

"I was worried sick about you and almost got a ticket on the way here because I wasn't paying attention to my speed. I see the turtleneck, let me see."

Linda slid down the turtleneck to show Robert the trace of bruising circling her neck. "That bastard, if ever I get my hands on him…"

"You are going to do nothing. I don't want anything to happen to you," Linda hugged Robert tightly.

"You don't know me; I will do it."

"I know you will, but he is not worth it."

"But, you, my dear, are very worth it," John was tall enough to see the windows to the back room at the exchange between Linda and Robert. He realized that there was much more going on than just a simple friendship. He wanted to give them their privacy, but needed the ticket labeler. They were re-tangled in a kiss and embrace so John knocked and coughed as he came to the back room and they broke apart quickly. They pulled apart, but Robert never let Linda's hand go, not wanting to be disconnected even for a second.

"Sorry. I need to get this. By the way, I didn't see anything or know anything," John said as he looked for the ticket labeler that was left in the back room.

Robert and Linda both laughed. When John finally left, Robert said, "Oh well, I guess we are found out."

"No, it's just John. He hates meddling, and he won't say anything. I will talk to him after you leave. What's the plan?"

"When do you get off work?"

"In about two hours, at 5:00 p.m. I want to go by the house to pick up the mail and check on things."

"You can't go alone. What is the address? If I am not there, do not go in the house, stay in the drive way until I get there."

"Yes, sir," Linda kind of smiled slightly saluting him to lighten the moment while she gave him the address of the house.

"I am serious."

"I know. I love it that you are so concerned about me."

"Okay, I am going to leave before I just hide out in the back and wait on you."

"No, I will be fine. You go ahead and I will call."

"I have got to have one more kiss and I will be on my way."

"With pleasure."

Robert said good bye to John as he was walking out the front door. Linda walked directly from the back to John.

"So, before you ask, Robert Matthews is a lawyer. He lived here and you should know him. We have reconnected since last week. It was nothing planned. It just happened. He is helping me through this process with James. I am not sneaking around and if you should know, a lot has happened since I came home. Know that I am getting a divorce as quick as possible and moving on with my life without James."

"I am not judging, Linda. I was just going to say that I hope that he makes you happy. I want you to be happy because I don't think that you've been happy for a long time. My biggest hope is that you are rid of James for good. I hate to tell you this, but I know that he has been cheating on you for a while."

"How do you know?"

"I came through your street one afternoon, taking something to my mom's friend, Ms. Patterson. I passed your house and saw James squeezing the behind of another woman."

"Through the front door!"

"Through the front door."

"Wow. Does everybody know that my husband is a cheater but me?"

"I don't know about everybody, but I saw it with my own two eyes. Just like I didn't want to see that my mom was holding me back, you didn't want to face up to what James was doing either. I don't want to pry but, did you ever think that he was cheating?"

"I did. I just had that feeling. I couldn't prove it. Everybody else could prove it, including my children, which is the worst. I was trying to protect them and now they are protecting me. What a turn of events."

"Be thankful that they are supporting you because they could be pressuring you to stay with their father. They are mature enough to know that even though he is their father, he is not what is best for you. Now, it will take a little time for them to accept Robert, but I believe that they will clearly see how happy he makes you and gladly receive him."

"I hope that you are right."

"I believe that I am. We only have about another hour to go, and then we are going to close up shop right at 5:00 p.m."

Linda and John worked the rest of the day with a rhythm of two people who had a lot on their mind but were determined to get a job done. At 4:45 p.m., the bell rang on the door, in came a young woman alone. John was in the back and Linda was out front ready to help her, "Can I help you?"

"Yes, is John Black here?"

"Yes, he is. Are you Grace?" Linda asked.

"Yes, I am," Grace answered somewhat puzzled.

"Hi, it is nice to meet you. My name is Linda. John has been smiling even more than normal and I hear that you are the reason." Grace smiled then as well.

"I don't know about that, but he makes me smile as well."

"Take good care of my friend. He is a great guy."

"I will do my very best." Just then John came from the back. "Linda, we had somebody donating some Christmas ornaments, do we want them out yet? Because Thanksgiving is just in a couple of weeks and..." John stopped short when he saw Grace. He smiled at the sight of her face and almost dropped the box.

"John, put the box on the front table before you drop it and take Grace in the back to talk or whatever," Linda smiled at her own comment. John put the box on the counter in Linda's reach. He took Grace's hand in his and led her to be back room. Just like Robert and Linda, when the door closed, he took Grace in his arms and gave her a warm kiss.

"Hey, how are you?"

"I am fine now. How are you?" They both laughed like teenagers.

"I am great now. Is everything alright?"

"Yes, I just wanted to see you. Is that alright?"

"That is perfect. I was going to stop by on my way home, but now you can go home with me. Do you have your car?"

"No, Marissa dropped me off, and I am all yours."

"Yes, you are. I will only be a few minutes, and then we will be ready to go. You want to wait back here or browse in the store."

"I will wait for you back here if that is okay," The bell rang again and in walked Jamie and David.

"Linda!"

"Jamie, it is so good to see you." The two women embraced as tight as sisters. Both women cried just a little at the thought of each of their losses.

"It is so good to see you too."

"I am so sorry to hear about your parents. I wish I could have been at the memorial service today. My prayers were with you."

"I think I could feel them. I am sorry, but this is David. He is an attorney with Robert Matthews' firm. As a matter of fact, I used to date him years ago. He has taken such great care of everything for me. I don't know what I would have done without him. This is my good friend and co-worker, Linda Sanders."

"Hi, David. It is good to meet you," Linda shook his hand and greeted him.

"So, you are Linda," David eyes lit up when he said the phrase.

"Yes, I am Linda." The two smiled and slightly nodded at each other. He wanted her to know that he knew about her relationship with his boss, Robert Matthews.

"Jamie, what are your plans the rest of the week? You have taken off, correct?" Linda asked.

"That is correct. I need the rest of the week to get my house in order to make some decisions. I am going to my apartment to check on things. David, and hopefully, Mr. Robert Matthews will meet with me this week to discuss some other options."

"Well, that is great. I hope that we can all see each other later this week as well. I have some decisions of my own to make. It is good to meet you, David."

"Likewise, I am here the rest of the week as well."

"Great. We are about to close the store and head out for the night. Jamie, get some rest and we shall talk soon."

"Good night, Linda, and thanks for your concern."

"Don't mention it. That's what friends are for," Linda said.

Jamie and David left the store. John and Grace came from the back of the store and John said, "Linda, get your stuff from the back while I put the key in the door."

Linda retrieved her things from the back and went out with Grace to wait on John. John set the alarm, flipped the switch on the lights and turned the key on the lock of the front door. John put Grace in his truck and watched as Linda got to her car. Darkness came early this time of the year. You couldn't be too careful. Linda started her car and called Robert.

"Hey, baby. You leaving now?" Robert answered on the first ring.

"Yes, love. I am on my way."

"Okay, I am leaving out now as well. Meet you there."

When Linda pulled in the driveway, Robert pulled in beside her. She got out of the car, went to the mailbox, got the newspaper off the porch and put the key in the door. When they walked in, Linda stopped short.

"You, okay?"

"No. This house has been violated as much as I have."

"What do you mean?"

"This was supposed to be a house of love, peace and joy. It has turned into a place of shame, hurt and embarrassment. When this is all said and done, I really want to sell it and move."

"You sure?"

"Yes, I am sure." Linda unlocked the door, but Robert opened the door and walked inside first. The house did not have a timer to activate the lights so the house was completely dark. Robert paused in the doorway for Linda to lead the way and turn on the lights in the living room and kitchen. They sat down at the kitchen table holding hands.

"What else?"

"Too many things. I need to figure out the status of the finances. If James' car was repossessed, what's the status of everything else, mortgage, utilities and savings? I have been so ignorant of so many things. I trusted him and went along with whatever he said to keep peace. I was so..."

"Stop that. I told you don't go back there. This is a new day. What else do you need me to help you take care of?"

"I need to get a divorce. I don't know if James is going to get out of jail soon or not. I need to talk to my sons about all of this. This is Stephen's senior year of high school. I don't want to interrupt that, but I don't want to stay here either. There are too many ghosts of James' trysts and escapades in this house for me to feel comfortable here. Do you know that my co-worker, John, saw James coming into this house squeezing the behind of another woman? He told me today. It seems like everybody knew and could prove it but, me. I think I suspected it on so many levels, but would never admit it." Robert's silence was comforting and reassuring for Linda. His concern was evident and he didn't mind Linda talking through this entire situation.

"When do you want to talk to your sons?"

"Soon. I am going to call William and see if he can come home this Friday and we will have a sit down with you," Linda said.

"Call him now," Robert insisted. Linda dialed the number.

"Hello," William answered on the first ring.

"Hello, William this is Mom. How are you, baby?"

"Fine Mom how are you? Is this your phone or did you borrow someone's?"

"This is my new phone. I am fine."

"Great, finally."

"Finally, is right. I need to know if you can come home after classes on Friday. I want you to meet Mr. Robert Matthews who is going to be my attorney. He is here this week and we are going to make plans with his guidance. Okay?"

"That's fine Mom. I think Ryan is coming home anyway, but I will check with him. Hold on. Ryan, are you going home on Friday?" 'Yeah man, we can go home if you need to,' is what Linda heard in the background.

"Tell Ryan I said, thank you. What time are you going to leave school?"

"We both get out at noon on Friday. We should be home at the latest by 3:00 p.m."

"Meet me at the house, because I am taking off early."

"Okay. I will be sure and program your number in my phone."

"Great. Has your brother called you yet?"

"Yes, he has. Mom?"

"Yes, baby?"

"I am so proud of you."

"Thank you. I am proud of me and you too. Goodnight baby," Linda started to cry.

"Goodnight mom," When Linda hung up, she went into Robert's welcoming arms to let out a good cleansing cry. It was also a cry of happiness from the love and support of her oldest son as well as a cry of victory to move on from James.

"Let it out, baby. It's okay."

"I don't know how it happened, but I have raised two wonderful young men. I am so thankful."

Linda and Robert closed up the house together, grabbed a bite to eat and said goodnight. As much as their bodies longed for each other, they used wisdom and went their separate ways. They had a lot to do over the days, weeks and months ahead. They vowed to stand together against any force that came to tear them apart. With another chance to be together, this time nothing would separate them.

On the other side of town, John and Grace made a similar commitment to one another, to love and live life to the fullest in the middle of his bed. They vowed to let nothing stop them from doing just that.

Over two plates of pancakes, Jamie and David agreed to go slow with their reconnected relationship, but let nothing come between them either. Jamie knew that she had a lot of issues to deal with about her parents, the new direction for her life but with David and his support, the primary direction would be up.

Chapter 15 – Next Steps...

Robert called David at 8:00 a.m. on Thursday.

"Hello."

"Good morning. I need your help on something. Linda Sanders is moving forward with the dissolution of her marriage to James Sanders, but needs to know a full financial disclosure. Can you find that out for her? He is currently locked up and shouldn't get out anytime soon if I can help it."

"Sure, I'll take care of it."

"Also, I am meeting with Harold Sanders this morning. He called me, so I don't know exactly what he wants, but I will soon find out at 10:00 a.m. We need a Dun & Bradstreet on his firm as well. If you need more info and can't get it all online, get the law librarians in Indianapolis to help you on it too."

"Fine."

"I will give you a call after the meeting and we can go over what we talked about and make some decisions of our own. We also need to take a look at the property where I want our offices to be located. Since we are here for the week, we should maybe pay a visit to our Louisville clients as well. See if you can arrange that for tomorrow morning. Nothing serious just a check in, stop by or lunch if they are available."

"Will do. I will text you since you are preparing for your meeting. Maybe we can get together this afternoon and maybe have dinner this evening sometime with Jamie and Linda," David said.

"Are you trying to set up a double date?" Robert asked.

David laughed an 'I'm busted' laugh and added, "Well, they mentioned it when I met Linda on yesterday."

"You saw Linda."

"Yes, I met her yesterday in the store with Jamie."

"What did you think?"

"I think that you are one lucky man. As long as she loves you as much as you love her, you'll be fine."

"How can you tell?"

"Man, your nose is so wide open for this woman. I think that you would move heaven and earth for her. Is she the one?"

"Yep, she's the one."

"Go for it. Fall head over heels. You are past due for great love in your life."

"Thanks man. So are you."

"We'll see about that. We have a lot of work to do. We are taking it slow."

"You are saying 'go slow' with your mouth to her, but your heart is already there."

"You are right. We'll talk later. How about 5:00 p.m. for dinner?"

"I will check with Linda."

"That sounds good."

"I liked the way that sounded to me too."

"Bye, sir."

"Goodbye, David." Robert smiled to himself. Robert arrived at Sanders & Associates at 9:50 a.m.

"Can I help you sir?" The receptionist said.

"I am Robert Matthews to see Mr. Harold Sanders."

"Yes, sir, right away." The receptionist called Mr. Sanders' secretary and stated that the visitor had arrived. Harold Sanders walked down the hallway from his office to the lobby to meet Robert personally.

"Robert," Harold Sanders spoke first.

"Hello, Harold." The two men shook hands looking each other straight in the eye. Harold led Robert back to his private office not speaking until he had closed his door.

"Have a seat. It appears that my son, James, has gotten himself in some big trouble. He slept with a minor and my grandson has the pictures to prove it. He called me and I told him that I won't bail him out. There is great tension in my household right now but, I will not go back on my word. He has a long road ahead of him. My second issue is I am sixty years old and ready to retire. I am done. I want your firm to take over my firm. We can work out all of the financials later. I just want to have the Sanders name on the door in some way, Matthews and Sanders, if you agree. I want this done by December 31st. I know it's fast, but I am ready. I am going to tell the staff at the company dinner on December 15th and would like for you to be there. Jim Parker is the senior attorney on staff. I am not going to tell you who should run the office, but I recommend him to you. He's knowledgeable, loyal to the firm, loves his wife and has a great family. His son, Ryan, has applied to law school and usually works for us in the summer as a runner. Finally, I need you to represent my daughter-in-law, Linda, against my son in her divorce or anything else she needs. I will pay the bill whatever it takes. I believe I owe her that. She is too nice a woman to have ever married my son. They were young. Some men are mostly dog and only part man, but my son is ALL dog and mostly boy. I am embarrassed and ashamed, but his mother spoiled him and I went along with it."

"Are you sure that your wife won't bail him out?" Robert asked.

"Yes, I am sure. She doesn't have a credit card or any money to bail him out of anything or anywhere. I control everything that goes on in our house."

"Okay, just checking. Well, since we are being honest here. If you remember, I used to date Linda. We have reconnected since I came back in town. I am going to represent her. But, know this, I am in love with Linda. I intend to marry Linda which I should have done years ago, if she will have me. By the way, did you know that your son tried to choke her to death? Your grandson, Stephen, stopped him, and she fell to the floor after he released his grip. I saw the marks around her neck as a result. I am furious with your son, and if I wasn't a member of the court, I would ask for a few minutes alone with James to knock him the hell out for what he has done to Linda and your grandsons. My goal, first and foremost, is her safety."

"I didn't know he choked her. I am so sorry. I totally understand your frustration with my son. I want to take a belt and beat him like he stole something out of my pockets. I had forgotten about you and Linda. I give you my whole hearted blessing in your relationship and future union. If you love like you do business, she won't say no. My son never loved her as she needed to be loved. It's not in him. You need to be a giver, to give love. My son is too selfish."

"Thank you and I appreciate your support. I am here the rest of the week as well as one of my associates. In addition to Linda's case, we are settling an estate and meeting with some other clients. Here is my cell number so you can call me day or night. I am going to be meeting with my associate right away to map out a strategy for your requests."

When Robert left Harold Sanders, he made two calls, Linda first.

"Hey, baby, would you mind having dinner with me, David and Jamie tonight around 5:00?"

"Everybody is here today except Jamie, let me see if I can leave early. Where are we going? Do I need to wear something nice?"

"As far as I am concerned, you can wear nothing at all."

"How would I look coming naked to dinner?"

"Good enough for me to eat on a plate."

"Dirty man. You know I like that," Linda remembered that naked dinner they shared at his place last weekend. Most of the food was eaten off of each other instead of the plates. 'Can't let my mind go there right now,' Linda thought.

"I love it, but we've got to get this business done so you can spend more time in my house and in my bed."

"In time, in time," Linda said smiling, "Hold on," Linda asked John if he could stay and lock up because she needed to leave early.

John agreed and said, "go ahead."

"Okay, love, John is going to lock up and I can leave here around 3:00 p.m. Where do you want me to meet you guys?"

"The Steakhouse on the highway. See you then. Bye, baby."

"Bye," Linda smiled even after she pressed 'end call.' Robert's next call was to David.

"Hello."

"David."

"Yes, sir."

"We are all set for the double date at 5 at the Steakhouse on the highway. I am headed back to the hotel and will be there in about 15 minutes. I will call you when I am in my room. You can let me know what information you found out since we spoke."

"Speak with you then."

Linda called Patty Parker at home. "Hello."

"Patty? This is Linda. I need another huge favor."

"Anything." Linda relayed her problem to Patty, and they agreed to take care of the problem at 3:30 p.m. when she got to her house.

Patty spun Linda around in her basement stylist chair toward the mirror. Linda couldn't believe it was her hair and face that she was seeing. Patty handed her a cute, sleeveless black dress with a mock. When she showered and put on the dress, Patty finished Linda's make-up.

Linda stood up and said, "Thank you Glam Squad. You have worked a miracle."

"Not a miracle. I just improved what you already had to work with. Go girl! You look gorgeous." The two hugged quickly as Linda was in a hurry. She put on her coat and was almost out the door when Stephen and Jason were coming in the house.

Stephen asked, "Hey Mom, where are you going?"

"To dinner with some friends."

"What friends?"

"Jamie from work, her lawyer and my lawyer."

"Dressed like that?"

"Yes, dressed like this."

"Well, you look good Mom."

"Thanks baby. You got your homework done?"

"Seniors don't have homework. We do it in study hall."

"Okay. Bye." Linda waved as she rushed out of the door.

Stephen walked in the bedroom and called his brother. Jason could only hear Stephen's side of the conversation. "I think Mom's got a boyfriend already. You should see the way she is dressed. I think it is the lawyer. We will both know tomorrow. See you then."

Linda arrived at the restaurant right at 5:00 p.m. Robert was already at the restaurant. He was looking out the window and started salivating, but it wasn't for the food. He was watching Linda walk across the parking lot. He had loved Linda's looks already and she didn't need to change a thing for him, but with her tall, slim build, new layered haircut, makeup and that dress! He wouldn't make it through dinner without hurting himself.

"Oh, baby, you look amazing. I am literally in pain right now," He whispered in her ear as they hugged at the door.

"Stop, Robert," Linda giggled playfully.

"No, I am not going to stop until you tell me to."

"Don't stop."

"That's what I thought," Linda giggled again. Robert made her smile and laugh more than ever.

"Baby, you are going to have to stay away from me. I feel like I am going to embarrass myself and get fully aroused if you get any closer."

"Are you for real?"

"I am so for real. You should feel under my coat." Linda looked both way as she ran her hand under the bottom button of his coat straight to his crotch and there was nothing left to the imagination.

"Oh my, Mr. Matthews. We have ourselves a big problem. Are they here yet?"

"No, they'll be here shortly. I just got a call from David."

"Sorry, I thought I could help you with that problem, but too late now, here they come." They were giggling when David and Jamie walked in the door. The night was wonderful. The four of them talked like old friends reconnecting. Good wine, good food and good company equaled a great time. They walked out of the restaurant around 9:00 p.m. Linda called Patty to leave the back door opened because she was going to have a night cap with Robert. The night cap turned into almost morning breakfast because she eased the back door open at 4:00 a.m. and the boys woke up for school at 5:30 a.m.

Patty came in to tease Linda after the boys left for school, "Girl, you took that dress for a spin, didn't you?"

"Yes, girl, and when I was finished, the dress was on the floor, and I was swinging from the chandelier." They both laughed.

"Girl, that's what I am talking about. That's the kind of relationship you want, hot, heavy and mutual."

"Right, now I am so sleepy."

"That's the way it is supposed to be. Loving that leaves you relaxed, sleepy and satisfied. The real good stuff. I will get you some caffeine while you take a shower."

"Thanks."

Linda went into work, but she was moving really slow. John commented first in a low tone, "Too much loving and late night I see. I think the kids call it creeping."

"Oh, shut up, John, you don't have kids so you don't have to creep. I do."

"That's okay. I will cover for you."

"Thanks." They both laughed.

During lunch, Jamie stopped by to say hi. Ms. Henrietta and Steve came in the store and to the back room to see everyone as well. Everybody was there so Ms. Henrietta said, "Excuse me everybody. Steve and I have an announcement. Go ahead baby."

"Baby?" everybody said in unison.

"Yes, baby," Ms. Henrietta said.

"Ms. Henrietta and I have been married since it became legal in 1967. We have decided to move from Roberts Junction."

"Married?" said Linda. "Why are you just now telling us?"

"Back when Henrietta came to work for me and my first wife, it was illegal for us to be together. We were lovers and had an affair for many years. We have three beautiful children together. We have a son that is a doctor in New York, a daughter who is a lawyer in Chicago and a daughter who is an engineer in Arizona. I was once the banker in Roberts Junction. One night I told my wife that I wanted a divorce and was going to live with Henrietta and take care of our kids together. She threw acid in my face. I was disfigured for some time. I went to live in Atlanta and had multiple surgeries. I lost my job at the bank, but had made some wise investments including buying a franchise in the Goodwill. This is my Goodwill and I own it."

"Wait a minute. When I was little, the banker was named Jefferson Walker. Why is your name Stephen Hamilton?" added John.

"Yes, I am Jefferson Walker, but after my surgery, my wife wanted to shame me in this town. I knew that Henrietta was still here and wanted to raise our children here, so I moved back here to be near her. I divorced my first wife, and with my new face, changed my name to Stephen Hamilton. Henrietta never took my name for fear of repercussion from my wife and her family. Henrietta and I have decided to move to Florida where it is warm and spend the rest of our days at our home there. John, I am asking that you manage the store. Will you take the job?"

"Sure but, it can't interfere with my retirement and pension, so I will have to tell you how much salary I can make right now."

"Great, because your first order of business will be hiring some new employees. From what I can tell from the back store video footage, Ms. Linda over there will not be here long."

"What did you see?"

"I am not telling, but you forgot about the cameras in the back as well as in the front of the store." Linda's face became red as crimson.

"Ms. Jamie, I suspect that you will be moving on with your life as well. I am really sorry to hear about your parents, but you have been hiding in Roberts Junction too long. Go find love, laugh and live your life. The Goodwill was a great place for you to stop over and regroup, but this can't be your final place to set down roots. You are too young. There is more for you to do."

"Thank you, Mr. Steve. I will be making that decision very shortly," Jamie replied.

"By the way, John, marry that girl I saw you on the camera with too. Good thing you guys are not childbearing age or she would be pregnant already."

Jamie yelled out, "Go John!"

John said proudly, "I am going to marry her right after Christmas. All are invited to the wedding. Just a small ceremony for those who love and support us."

"Invite your mom, life's too short. She might surprise you," Linda said.

"Thanks Linda, I will."

"Society shamed Henrietta and me for our love for so long that we hid it but no more. We have been together for more than forty years. We are not getting any younger and we could die anytime. We are about to live our best life with the days we have left. We hereby are giving our two weeks' notice. Here are the keys, John, and you have the combination to the alarm. We will talk salary on Monday. Let's go Henrietta."

"Goodbye everybody. Love you all," Steve and Henrietta walked out the Goodwill front door.

"Jamie, I need a big favor?" Linda asked, "I have to meet with Robert and the boys today at 3:00 p.m. Can you stay and help out John until close for me?"

"I would be honored. Let me call David and tell him that I won't be free for dinner until after 5:00 p.m." Jamie made her quick call and all was settled. Jamie and Linda worked together until 2:30. She arrived at home 15 minutes later to Robert and William talking at the kitchen table.

"Hey, baby, how long you been here?" Linda said. Not thinking, Robert and William both answered.

"About fifteen minutes." They all laughed which released some of the tension in the house.

"Oh," was all that Linda could say.

Stephen walked in about 5 minutes later.

"Mom, where are you guys?"

"In the kitchen, Stephen."

They were all here. The most important people in her life all under one roof.

"Anybody thirsty?" Linda said, but Stephen jumped up at the same time.

"Mom, sit down. I'll get everybody a bottle of water. You don't have to serve us anymore."

"Thank you," Linda watched as Stephen retrieved bottles of water for everyone and sat down next to her at the table.

Robert started the meeting. "My name is Robert Matthews. I own Matthews & Associates which has an office in Indianapolis and soon here in Roberts Junction and next in Louisville. I have known your mom and dad for more than twenty-five years. I will be honest. I dated your mom in high school. I made a huge mistake, and she broke up with me. She married your dad and I saw her last week when I walked in the Goodwill store to buy some shirts. I am in love with your mother. I loved her twenty-five years ago and I love her even more today. In high school, I had a baby by another woman and I have a daughter. My daughter is Jennifer who lives near her mother. Her mother is married to someone else and has more kids. I have never been married."

"Do you want to marry our mother?" Stephen asked.

"Yes, I want to marry your mother, if she will have me. But first, we have to settle things between your mother and father."

"Given everything that has happened and what I have found out recently, I want a divorce immediately from your father. He doesn't love me and I don't love him. He is in jail. Apparently, neither your grandfather nor your grandmother is going to bail him out. I want your opinion before I make any big moves so that's why we are here. Next, I am having a hard time thinking about staying in this house but, this is your house too. Do you think I should try to stay here or sell it?" Linda said.

William and Stephen both said, "Sell it!"

"You sure?"

"We are sure."

"Next, we have to find a place to live so Stephen can graduate from Cedar Ridge since this is his senior year."

"I can live with the Parkers. Mom, you go live with Mr. Matthews and start your life away from Roberts Junction. When I graduate, I will be going to IU and be with William until he goes to law school," Stephen said.

"Stephen, you are assuming a lot. You are assuming that Mr. Matthews wants me to live with him."

"Mom, he loves you. Of course he wants you to live with him."

"You are exactly right, Stephen. I would love for your mom to live with me. I love her more than she even knows," Robert turned from Stephen to look directly into Linda's face.

Linda wiped her face to catch the one tear and recovered fast enough to say, "Well, what about the Parkers? I haven't asked them about you staying there and I need to get their permission."

"I have already asked permission to live with them until I graduate."

"When was this?"

"When I saw you leave in that dress the other night," Stephen said. They all laughed. Linda blushed. Robert closed his eyes to try to focus and not be reminded of that dress. Just thinking about making love to Linda for those six hours made his body long for her even now and he was supposed to be in a meeting.

"Wow, Stephen, as always, you are intuitive and bold to say the least. I would just feel more comfortable asking them myself. I don't want it to seem like I am abandoning you or leaving you on their doorstep," Linda added.

"Mom, I am seventeen years old and will be eighteen long before I graduate. I am too big to leave on a doorstep. I want to graduate from Cedar Ridge with all of my friends and I promise not to be any problem to the Parkers. I will come and visit during the holidays. We can arrange that." They all smiled at Stephen's statements.

"That's another question, too. Where are we going to spend the holidays?" Linda asked.

"You can stay at my house. It is big enough for everybody, including the Parkers," Robert said.

"William, you haven't said anything. What's going on in your mind?"

"Mom, I am good with everything. I already said my peace to Mr. Matthews before you came in. I know that I can stay with the Parkers when I come home from school. I want Mr. Matthews to love you the way you are supposed to be loved, take care of you like you deserve and spoil you rotten. I can tell that you care about him."

"Why?" Linda asked.

"You cut your hair and starting to care about yourself. Dad took that from you. Mr. Matthews is giving that back to you including a cell phone. You have always taken care of us, but it is now time for us to take care of you."

"Okay, I am not going to ask any more questions. This is the plan; first Mr. Matthews or Robert is going to help me get a divorce. Second, we start packing tomorrow to move and sell the house. I will speak with the Parkers. I will move with Robert, to Bloomington. What I am going to do there I don't know? I will figure that out when the time comes. I love the three of you more than you know. I have a lot to face, but I know I will make it with the three of you on my side." Linda said as she looked into the face of Stephen, William and finally Robert. They were all smiling back at her for added assurance.

"Make that four!" Harold Sanders came through the kitchen door. "Sorry to barge in, but you left the front door open."

"Hey, Harold. Why are you here?" Linda asked.

"I wanted to come and make sure you knew how upset I am about the way my son has treated you and my grandsons. I am furious about his behavior. I am not going to get him out of jail. If he tries to get out, I will help prosecute him myself.

I am glad to see that Robert Matthews is your representative as well as someone who loves and cares for you very much. I am here to pay for everything. What can I help you do?"

"I am filing for divorce. Stephen is going to stay here and graduate from Cedar Ridge and live with the Parkers."

"Stephen, if you need anything, I am a phone call away."

"Yes, sir."

"I am going to sell the house and move with Robert to Bloomington."

"Linda, I will buy the house and rent it out for you. If you want to leave it furnished that would be easier to rent as well. You let me know when your personal items are out of here and we can start the process of interviewing renters. I am retiring as of December 31st and selling the firm to Robert. We have not finalized all of the details yet but, we will come to an agreement no matter what. I want to leave it in his hands."

"Robert, are you going to be moving here?" Linda asked.

"No, we may have a temporary company apartment here, but I am not going to build a permanent home here. I am going to have Jim Parker in charge of the office here and help me start an office in Louisville. David will be in charge of the office in Indianapolis. After the beginning of the year, I want to take six months off so that Linda and I can travel and enjoy each other. I really want to teach at IU and UofL in the Fall when we return. I will stay on as a consultant/managing partner with the new Matthews and Sanders Firm. I have worked very hard over the past two decades, but it now time to turn my passion for the law into the passion for Linda. Agree, Linda?"

"Totally agree Robert. I am so overwhelmed by how my life has changed in one week, I can't speak," Linda turned toward her sons and father-in-law as she continued, "I want you all to know that I was dead, but this man's love has brought me back to life. I am ready to live. Do I have your permission?"

"Mom, you don't need our permission, but you have our blessing. Please be happy and enjoy your life," Stephen and William said while smiling at their mother.

"Congratulations, Linda. We have much to iron out, Robert. I am proud of my family now and know that our future is bright with these young men and you guiding them forward." Harold Sanders said.

New Life

Over the next few months, William went back to school at IU to finish out his sophomore year with honors. Stephen graduated in the top of his high school class while living with the Parkers. John married Grace on New Years' Day and John's mother was present to meet her new granddaughter and great grandson. Jamie and David began a new life in Indianapolis. Jamie enrolled at Indiana University/Purdue University to study Graphic Design and Communications. Linda settled all of her business in Roberts Junction and began her new life being loved and spoiled rotten by Robert Matthews. Linda married Robert on Christmas Eve the following year. Henrietta and Steve never returned to Roberts Junction. They lived in Florida during winter but, spent time at each of their children's homes the other three seasons until they died. All of this love and life was once hidden in Roberts Junction.

More Books from Kadance Royal